DOG PEOPLE

A novel

by

Peter Beere

and

Garry Kilworth

Dedications

PB - This is for Marti, who kept the faith.

GK - In memory of Dylan, my Wychwater companion.

Other books by Garry Kilworth

Novels
Witchwater Country
Spiral Winds
Standing on Shamsan
The Iron Wire

Science Fiction Novels
In Solitary
The Night of Kadar
Split Second
Gemini God
Theatre of Timesmiths
Cloudrock
Abandonati

Fantasy Novels
Hunter's Moon
Midnight's Sun
Frost Dancers
House of Tribes
Roof of Voyaging
The Princely Flower
Land of Mists
Highlander (novelisation of film script)
A Midsummer's Nightmare
Shadow-Hawk

Young Adults' Books
The Wizard of Woodworld
The Voyage of the Vigilance
The Rain Ghost
The Third Dragon
The Drowners
Billy Pink's Private Detective Agency

The Phantom Piper
The Electric Kid
The Brontë Girls
Cybercats
The Raiders
The Gargoyle
Welkin Weasels Book 1 – Thunder Oak
Welkin Weasels Book 2 – Castle Storm
Welkin Weasels Book 3 – Windjammer Run
Welkin Weasels Book 4 – Gaslight Geezers
Welkin Weasels Book 5 – Vampire Voles
Welkin Weasels Book 6 – Heastward Ho!
Drummer Boy
Hey, New Kid!
Heavenly Hosts v Hell United
The Lantern Fox
Soldier's Son
Monster School
Nightdancer
Faerieland Book 1 – Spiggot's Quest
Faerieland Book 2 – Mallmoc's Castle
Faerieland Book 3 – Boggart and Fen
The Silver Claw
Attica
Jigsaw
Hundred-Towered City

Horror Novels
The Street
Angel
Archangel

Short Story Collections
The Songbirds of Pain
In the Hollow of the Deep-sea Wave
In the Country of Tattooed Men
Hogfoot-right and Bird-hands

Moby Jack and Other Tall Tales
Tales from the Fragrant Harbour
Dark Hills, Hollow Clocks
Phoenix Man – 13 Eclectic Tales
The Fabulous Beast

Fantasy Novels as Kim Hunter
The Red Pavilions Book 1 – Knight's Dawn
The Red Pavilions Book 2 – Wizard's Funeral
The Red Pavilions Book 3 – Scabbard's Song

Historical Fantasy Novels as Richard Argent
Winter's Knight

Historical Sagas as FK Salwood
The Oystercatcher's Cry
The Saffron Fields
The Ragged School

Historical War Novels
Jack Crossman series
The Devil's Own
Valley of Death
Soldiers in the Mist
The Winter Soldiers
Attack on the Redan
Brothers of the Blade
Rogue Officer
Kiwi Wars

Ensign Early series
Scarlet Sash
Dragoons

Memoirs as Garry Douglas Kilworth
On my way to Samarkand: memoirs of a travelling writer
Rookie Biker in the Outback

Other books by Peter Beere:

Trauma 2020 Series:

Urban Prey
The Crucifixion Squad
Silent Slaughter

The Squad Series
The Squad
The Fifth Man
The Sixth Day

Young Adult
Crossfire
Underworld
Underworld II
Underworld III
School for Death
Kiss of Death
Doomsword
Star Warriors
At Gehenna's Door
Riot

Younger Readers
Bod's Mum's Knickers
The Locked Door (A play)

Reviews

'Peter Beere is funny, he's acerbic, and he has terrific insight into the human heart.'
Gillian Philip

'Peter Beere's unflinching eye and Noirish humour remind me of Jo Nesbo at his very best.'
Celia Rees

IN SOLITARY: Kilworth's characters are strong and the sense of place he creates is immediate. (Sunday Times)

THE SONGBIRDS OF PAIN is excellently crafted. Kilworth is a master of his trade. (Punch Magazine)

SPIRAL WINDS: A subtle, poetic novel about the power of place - in this case the South Arabian Deserts - and the lure of myth. It haunted me long after it ended. (City Limits Magazine)

ABANDONATI: Full of hope, irony and despair and as moving in its understated way as Riddley Walker, the last post-apocalypse novel worth paying hard cash for. (Time Out Magazine)

WITCHWATER COUNTRY: Atmospherically overcharged like an impending thunderstorm. (The Guardian)

IN THE COUNTRY OF TATTOOED MEN: A masterpiece of balanced and enigmatic storytelling . . . Kilworth has mastered the form. (Times Literary Supplement.)

DOG PEOPLE: ONE

1991

The first time I saw the squatters they weren't actually inside the house. They were in my garden, close to the trees. I have a large garden, and it runs on a slope from south to north and at the top of the slope lies a wood which covers slightly more than an acre. The wood holds a pond which is now largely stagnant having gathered leaves from many autumns, and the squatters were midway between the dead pond and the lawn's edge, a distance of about twenty yards from me. They were standing, not doing anything, just looking at the house. I could see that they'd built a small fire for themselves. As I turned the key in the lock of my front door I remember thinking how good it was to smell woodsmoke. The smell of a campfire in early winter seems to have more fragrance to it than at any other time of the year. I wondered what they were using. Hickory? Oak? Whatever it was there was more smoke than flame, and could not have been very warming.

It was a late November evening and it was cold outside the house, but the strangers appeared not to notice it. Perhaps they were toughened from living like campers, or having no choice, they just ignored it. Whatever their reasons, there were three of them out there: two men and a woman, and the female was heavily pregnant. I remember thinking at the time: *she shouldn't be out there in her condition, she's likely to do herself an injury.* But for all my concern the woman herself seemed contented, if contentment could be the right word for it. I suppose, most of all, the woman seemed *peaceful*, standing within the shifting shadows, hands hugging herself underneath the great bulge while the light from the fire flickered over her. She appeared, yes, she seemed to be almost content. But I have to say 'almost' because, although that was my impression of *her*, the two men seemed tense, their movements were brittle. She could not be in the company of two such taut males and be completely at ease in her own mind.

I think it must have been the appearance of contentment which prevented me from actually doing anything. I suppose I really should have done something: they had invaded my garden, they had built a potentially dangerous fire in my brambles and deadwood and hazels. God knows what damage they could have caused. They could have broken into my shed and stolen the tools. They could have used the croquet mallets for kindling.

But they seemed so goddamned *peaceful* out there. It seemed such a shame to disturb them.

I went out a little later, when a frost was beginning to creep down the hill, and carefully unlocked the shed. If they were going to break into it, I didn't want them damaging the door but, also, I did not want to provoke them.

I don't know how long they had been in the wood, I don't think they were there when I left for work that morning, which would have been about eight o'clock.

I put the exterior lamp on at about nine p.m. and its bright light flooded across the lawn until it became lost in the first stand of trees. The squatters moved towards it, like moths. They fluttered around in its brightness for a while, then went back to their fire. I wasn't worried by them, by the fact that they were just strangers who'd camped in my garden. Three strangers who stared at my house. There's not much to damage out there and I'm no possessive landowner, jealous of the footprints of others on my clay. The loam was there before I came, and will remain afterwards. You don't take the soil with you when you go: the soil claims you. So, despite these estate managers and farmers who claim ownership to the earth, there's little to be excited about in my opinion. A garden doesn't belong to us, we belong to it.

Strangely, I didn't feel *personally* threatened, either. If you had asked me about it beforehand, I would have said, yes, there would be something threatening about people in your garden, three strangers who stared at your house. I think my first answer would be, ring the police, get the squatters removed right away. But, not being menaced, I didn't think of calling anyone, and this could have been my major mistake. I don't know really what I felt to be honest, but certainly not uneasy, and not even afraid of them. I think that what I felt mostly, was embarrassment.

I suppose they stared at me as well, for I stood at the window of my bedroom looking down on them. I had a whisky and soda in my hand and something was playing on the stereo behind me, though I forget what it could have been now. Something soft and soothing I imagine. Something for the November darkness.

I suppose that if I had been living with someone, I would have turned to them and said, 'There are people camping out in our garden,' and they would have undoubtedly suggested or insisted that I do something about it. But I wasn't living with anyone, I was on my own, and my reactions were totally different. I might have been enraged in company, if only because that would have been expected of me. I might have been indignant on the other person's behalf and I might have gone out and confronted the squatters, or at least shouted something from the window. We often do what we think we should do, and we sometimes don't think for too long on it.

No, I remember it now, the music wasn't soothing. It was cruel and demonic and probably rolled out across the lawn until it got lost with the squatters. There would be no one else to detect it beyond them and perhaps that is why they were looking at the house. Perhaps I had disturbed their evening.

What *should* one do when three strangers move in and blithely take over one's garden? Should one take one's old shotgun out of its gun case, and stand at the window and brandish it? Should one bark like a dog, in order to make the intruders believe there is a Doberman, or an Alsatian in the house? Most people are terrified of savage dogs. Perhaps I should have crouched down on all my four limbs and run, snarling and snapping at them?

But I did none of those things. I did nothing at all. I just stood at the window and watched them, as they stared at me.

While I was doing so I saw them go over to the stagnant pond and fish out some water. They put an old tin can to boil on the fire, and one of the three, the woman I think, gathered up some items from under the trees and stirred them into the pot. I couldn't see what it was she was collecting: the fire had died to a glow. I thought it must be some old hazelnuts, because there would not be too much else out there. Maybe a crab apple or two, but the squirrels had eaten most of them. And then a soft ringing distracted me. The sound of the telephone.

Monica's voice said, 'Do I put the wine in first, or the Emmenthal?'

I sipped my drink, still staring out of the window.

'Well?' she said, with impatience flooding down the line like a river of fire.

'What?' I said.

'I'm making a fondue. Do I put the wine in first, or the cheese?'

'The wine' I answered, and Monica hung up. She is a mistress of fluttering phone calls.

The wind was rising outside. Although I couldn't feel it myself, it looked like a November wind with a sharp cutting edge. The wind whistles in through the flat Essex marshes, all the way from Siberia, with nothing to blunt it before it starts scything at my trees. The squatters were roaming about, picking up branches and feeding them to the small fire. But it was growing no larger; if anything it appeared to be fading. After a few moments I pushed open the window and said, 'There are some logs over there.' And I pointed. But they did not seem to hear me.

The rising wind was whipping sparks from the top of their guttering fire. It seemed they were engaged in a desperate battle to prevent it from flattening out. But they moved very slowly, for they must have realised it was a terribly long night ahead of them. They had to hang on to their energy. They were like dark phantoms in my woodland. The tall, bearded one had a thin hollow face, as if it had been scooped out at some time. The other man, the smaller male, had much rounder features, but they were entirely expressionless. Not stamped on with misery, just devoid of all statement, so that only the woman seemed to have any animation and I think she smiled once, but I could have been mistaken. She might have done nothing at all.

Their shadows danced slowly like a tribe of the damned, in and out of leafless trees, across the darkened grass.

After a time, as if their dancing exhausted me, I turned from the window and slept on my bed. And in the morning, when I looked out across the frost-whitened lawn, the squatters appeared to have gone.

DOG PEOPLE: TWO

I was late at the office the following day (the day after the squatters' arrival). It was not through any fault of mine, the train delayed, it dragged its heels, it hung fire, its heart remained in Rochford. Such delays are not infrequent, and although I never fail to compensate the firm for loss of time there is a very specific air of disapproval which accompanies me from the lobby to my desk, an air which might accompany one who has inherited great wealth while others must toil for their pleasures; and an air which, if it were to be seen in its colours, would be a cruel and acidic shade of green. And yet I have ceased to offer explanations, nor do I tender excuses, for at the end of the day, and all things considered, it is only a job in an office. It does not give power to change water into wine, nor indeed, to breathe life into the dying.

And there was another reason why I was late, but one I could not have explained to them. Not far from the office I passed a particular car and as always a cold fury washed through me. Since the street it was left in was practically empty I crossed over and stood for a time looking at it. There was a lot of time left to elapse on the parking meter, so I assumed the owner would be gone a while. That gave me a chance to kick at the door panel until there was a sizeable dent in it. The radio aerial had been retracted, so I settled for ripping off one of the mudflaps and flinging it over a fence. Then a woman appeared with a skip round the corner and I walked away quickly, shaking my head and tutting as if I had just seen the habit of vandals, and was ashamed for the whole human race. I didn't look back, for there would be other cars to wreck, although I am not a professional wrecker.

I was a little tired for this was a bad day, for any one of a number of reasons. It was a bad day because one of the firm's deceased clients had been dishonest, or stupid, or just simply ignorant, and I was the one who had wound up his loose ends so it was upon me that the greatest rocks fell. Of itself that could have been enough to have tainted the entire day from the outset, but what made it worse, and what really gave it anger, was the terrible acknowledgement that, no matter what others thought, I just couldn't give a God-damn about it. I think that this rather got to irritate some people, and it almost got to irritate me. (Certainly it raised up at least one man's hackles, the hackles of Malcolm J Barnett.)

He hove in on me like a beaching whale as I threw myself down at my desk with a beaker of coffee. His shadow preceded him, for he is a large man, and one is enveloped in shade if he lingers. He was sweating profusely, but that's not unusual for Malcolm J Barnett's an oleaginous character who produces perspiration which is close to the consistency of margarine. It goes with his three surplus stones and his pallid skin, and that surplice which he calls a shirt.

'What's up, Malc?' I said, taking a blast of the fear scent which goes hand in hand with his cloying sweat; for Malcolm J Barnett will die for the workplace and, in fact, has almost no life beyond it.

He blurted, 'The Revenue's got hold of the Adams case, they're opening the Surtax assessments.' His blue eyes were frantic; were small, pale and frantic; like tropical fish in a milk-bowl.

'Don't be ridiculous,' I said. 'The man's dead and buried. Surtax went out fifteen years ago.'

'They're already doing it,' he said. He sat on my desk, with the flesh of his bottom rolling down and beneath the desk's lip. It was morbidly fascinating and I wondered how many women he must have smothered when he eased into love-games. None, I imagined, for who could indulge in a session with a mountain of butter? 'Unreported foreign dividends,' he went on. 'Australian income, and something about names of convenience.'

'What does that mean?' I said. 'Names of convenience? What kind of unreported dividends?'

'They're talking about eighty thousand pounds,' he said. 'Interest and penalties. It's already listed.'

I lit a cigarette to buy time. 'They can't list a case without consulting us. And what the hell are these 'names of convenience'? It doesn't even make sense to me.'

'I don't know,' he said. 'It's the term that they used. We're really in the crap-heap on this one. You'd better sort it out by lunchtime, Franklyn is wanting a report.'

'What report? There's nothing in the file. His widow isn't living in the country. She's living in France now, she's living with her daughter. She isn't even available for contact.'

'I can't help that,' said Malcolm J, dripping like rain on my blotting paper. I watched with revulsion as the rancid blobs blossomed and spread into ragged wet suns. 'You'd better come up with something,' he muttered. And on that note he left for his own desk, greatly relieved that he'd passed on the buck, and that I was the poor sucker he'd dumped it on. I tore off the top sheet of wet blotting paper and stuffed it into a wastebin, removing at least that much of him from my desk, for Malcolm J leaves his excretions all over the place; nail parings, hair cuttings, traces of sweat and dead skin; he performs his ablutions out in the open, messing around with a pair of small scissors, mopping himself all over with tissue. He never stops, he's like an exhibition of his own detritus, he has spread himself all over London and the South East of England. I suspect that it's his bid to achieve immortality, for there's very little else that he could leave us. Some people leave books or great works of their art behind, or some leave a statue in a park somewhere. Some even leave a few grandchildren in their wake, but Malcolm just leaves us these scraps of himself. It's one crazy legacy for future generations, they'll scratch a few heads over that one.

I tried hard to put Malcolm out of my mind and looked at the file of Felix Adams. He was a man who died over two years ago now, and I had the task of exhuming him.

'Names of convenience.' What the hell's that one? I've never heard them use that in the past. Mickey Rooney? Theodore Roosevelt? They seemed convenient to me. But then again, what about 'Swiss Cottage Public Toilets'? Do you think that's convenient enough, Malcolm?

It was a dull and thankless search through the file of an estate that had already been wound up. After a while I sat staring out of the window, because it seemed the most interesting thing I could do. I have a pain which often starts at times like this. It begins in my stomach then inches its way up my gullet and peaks around my tonsils. It's a constant pain; that is to say it comes and goes with metronomic efficiency and varying levels of hatred. If I am filled with stress the hate is vicious. At moments of tension it can be a dull anger. When I am nervous it mutters my name to me. I know every inch of its passage so well I can pinpoint positions by watching a clock. But on this day my despiser had chosen to ignore me, my tormentor slept deep in my stomach.

It was no miracle cure for a condition that is inevitably ulcerous. (I shouldn't drink but, oh my god, how do I get through these lonely days sober?) Nor was it a delayed condition in which even the anticipation of pain can prove painful. It was just that my stomach, like my brain, couldn't be bothered. There were better things to give up my peace for.

Adams was dead. I knew the Inland Revenue was not going to haul his asthmatic incontinent wife back from France so she could fork out another few thousand. So was it my role to take on an ulcer for nothing? On that day, I thought that it wasn't. As I've said, it was one of those bad days. You might as well stay in your rock pile.

It irritated Malcolm J that I couldn't join in with his grief; but I know my worth, and I know what my life is worth, and it has to be worth more than that. So it transpired that by lunchtime I had still made no progress, and I went for a walk around Finsbury Circus and ate my cheese sandwiches alone. Before I left the office I'd put in a call to Monica, but she was locked up in a meeting. Instead, I talked to her secretary, Pamela, who's really more fun but she isn't my type. (For one thing she's awesomely cheerful.) Between us we make a kind of unfinished triangle. Monica loves me (says she loves me), I am half in love with both of them, and Pamela loves like an exploding puff ball, giving it out in all directions. I think that if maybe we all got together we could work something out in this madness. But I kind of like abstracts so maybe it's better if the triangle is rather wonky. I may have to think about that one some day. But not on a grim day like this.

I roamed around the Circus, and looked at the people out walking. There is a tramp there, a permanent resident, who keeps one tiny area spotlessly clean, as if he had his own living-room and had become like a housewife, a Mrs Ogmore-Pritchard of the city. I sometimes would buy him cups of tea from the stand, or give him the last of my sandwiches. He would snatch them from me, shouting, 'I don't want your sandwiches! Don't want your bloody free handouts!' and he'd angrily wave me off. Then he would slope off himself with whatever I had given him, and drink it or eat it out of sight.

Today I gave vent to all my anguish, pouring it out onto anyone who would stand still and listen. The poor tramp just gaped at me, fish-eyed and frog-mouthed, and nervously scuttled away. I had broken the first of our unspoken contracts; I had behaved as I'm not supposed to.

Beside my pain, I have a nightmare through my waking hours. It has a name, but I don't like to talk of it; and it has a colour, which I'll name, which is black. Black is the colour of emptiness and loneliness, not the colour of solitude, which is white. White is the blanket which lies on all colours, and solitude is not a bad thing. I live alone and, at my work, where time is money, seconds count, in an office of twenty there is poor interaction, and no one can be quite alone. That is my solitude, that space and that liberty, the freedom not to interact.

So solitude does not disturb me. But then, its black counterpart does.

I have not always lived alone. I had a wife, I had a son. They both died when my wife drove her Escort 1.3 LX (central locking, powered mirrors) into a tree on the A127, Eastern Avenue, the Arterial as it is known locally. Perhaps she intended to drive into a tree, I don't know; what I do know is that the impact of the crash was far reaching, it fractured my life, it punctured a hole in it. Thereafter, there were not only cracks in my existence, there was a terrible weight of loneliness and a crushing emptiness, which combined together to give me the nightmare which haunts me. This is the blackness I don't put a name to. And this is why, sometimes, I don't think I act quite the same. (Although, I know that on some days I'm better.)

This was the day that my family was killed on, in a car crash, on this day a year ago.

Do you know how that can affect you? Picture this: you are walking along a street, perhaps you are in Finsbury Park, and you look up at the sky because it is a very bright day. Buildings rise around you, tall and white, and at the top of their pillars or arches or curlicues you see clusters of pigeons in their slate and blue uniforms, and you know they are making those soft pigeon noises, and the fat puffed-out male birds are eyeing the females (never stopping, rain or shine, for pigeons know life is a mess) and they are doing the things that birds do. Beyond and above them you see a blue sky with rolling clouds like smoke in a jungle, and way up high you see a plane, a silver dart on vital missions, as clear as a mote in your eye. And then, upon the sweep of the sky, across the clouds, above the pigeons, you see the faces of your family looking directly down on you. Huge faces covering the heavens.

How do you cope with a moment like that? How do you relate that to the fact that back at the office a fat man is grieving because another fat man threw a curve at a time when he was probably already dying from the cancer that killed him? Is it worth breaking out in a sweat for?

I don't know, I suppose that for some people it must be. Me, I get my sweats elsewhere: from seeing images that shouldn't be there. It's not the first time I've experienced a hallucination (call it what you like) but it's the first time those faces were *looking* at me. This is not a good experience at all.

I miss my family, but not in the sense that I have a perpetual loss, for one comes in some way to accommodate that. What is hard to come to terms with is the fact that you're somebody else now. You look back and those people are strangers to you: even the husband and father. Their deaths marked the moment of change. All three died. Two behind the wheel of a car, and one later, in the stark emptiness of his home.

The only way I can handle this is to believe that all three of them really are gone, and they're not hanging around somewhere (like up in the heavens) witnessing my usurper betray all those hand-me-down memories. And I pray that there isn't an afterlife.

That is the frame of mind I was in that day when I saw the vision in the sky and smelled the fear sweat of Malcolm J Barnett. I should have stayed at home that day, but there the ghosts were greater, they had entry. But I could not work, I could not function on that level, and though I'd planned for the day I was still not prepared for it, when it eventually came. I could not prepare for the anniversary of death. I had never been given instruction.

And most of all, the greatest anguish was that I did not truly grieve, not in the sense that I thought I would. I hardly even missed them. It was the date that stole the glory, like a birthday. But what were the changes? I couldn't put a name to them. I was still the same man yesterday. I will still be the same man tomorrow.

I took a longer than usual lunch because I knew that Franklyn was awaiting my report and if one must sin one should do it as bravely as possible. Nobody loves a loser, but they hate the half-hearted even more. I stayed out until three o'clock, by which time Franklyn would be 'visiting a client', which is his euphemism for jumping into bed with a Jewish prostitute he frequents every Tuesday and Friday.

While I walked I ran scenarios through my head. In the morning Franklyn would request my report and in his cluttered office, with the shelves full of cacti, I would offer some plausible excuse. But they all came out wrong. I started with abuse and became more insulting with each sentence, until in one scene I actually killed him. (It was the only moment in the day when I felt like laughing). I stabbed Bernard Franklyn through the left eye with the bronze letter-opener he brought back from Guernsey, and a state of catatonic shock travelled along his optic nerve and froze his brain. Then I trampled on all his cacti. Shortly after that, Malcolm J burst into the room. That was as far as I got.

The car hit a tree on the A127.

The stump stands like a tombstone today.

I had been back in the office for almost an hour when a call came in on the external line. A voice at the other end said, 'Where do you keep the washing powder?'

'I beg your pardon?' I said.

'Where do you keep the washing powder?'

I looked at the phone as though it was stupid, then my eyes slowly looked around the office.

'Who's that calling please?' I said.

But there was no reply. After a few moments the phone went dead.

I put the receiver back in its cradle and sat for a few moments debating what had happened. My debate did not lead anywhere.

I could not think any more about it until I got home that night.

DOG PEOPLE: THREE

I am a terrible insomniac. One of the reasons for this might be that I tend to fall asleep on the train, going and coming from work. Or it could be that I sleep at other times, without actually being aware of it. Malcolm J will tell you I am rarely awake, but he enjoys clichéd sneers like no other person I know. He uses them as handkerchiefs to collect all the dirt which accumulates inside his head.

Anyway, whatever the reason, I have trouble getting to sleep at nights. If I go past midnight I usually turn on the radio, channel four, and wait for the late shipping bulletin. The man who reads the shipping forecast (or bulletin, I don't know which) has a calm reassuring voice. I think they chose him for his soft, firm tones. When a terrible storm is imminent, out in the Bay of Biscay, the trawler captains need to be told in such a way that they do not run around in black panic. They need a calm voice full of confidence to anchor them to their reason as the white water climbs in mountains above them, before crashing down on the bows, scouring the decks clear of anything that hasn't been lashed down. I was once told by a merchant seaman that those who do not go out on the high seas have no real idea of the strength of the water. He said there are waves which can bend iron pillars and crush a man's body to pulp. He said you cannot begin to oppose such a power, you only go with it, like a cork: and the force takes you where it might want.

Only the rationally insane go out into seas that would freeze a man's muscles to a standstill in seconds; into winds that would strip the paint from a bowsprit; in waters that turn into foaming giants within an hour of setting off from a port.

So, it is to the shipping forecast man that I turn in my hours of need, when thoughts become cyclic and I can't rid my head of some trivial mistake which corrupts in the dark hours of night. Or when some dread has fallen on me which I cannot quite shake off. I need such a person to dispel the anxiety. The same man has been reading the bulletin since I was a child: at least, it still *sounds* like it is the same man. Perhaps they train each other before they are replaced, so that the radio officers in the merchant marine are further assured by continuity. They can spin the dials of their receivers and recognise the voice in an instant:

.' . .Faroes – North by Northeast – Clear – 1005 – rising. Finistere – North by Northwest – Drizzle – 7 miles – 1002 – Rising more slowly.'

I feel that the night world is safe in his hands. There is nothing to shake his authority. I can go to sleep and leave it all to him. And usually I do.

Sometimes he ends his broadcast, *'Goodnight, Gentlemen, and good sailing.'* I rarely hear the end, because by that time I'm asleep. I wake, later on, in the early hours to switch the radio off, and remove the buzzing from my ear.

Because I do not sleep habitually well I am perpetually tired, and seldom feel fully awake.

That's how I felt when I got home that night, dragging myself up the slope towards the house. I could see a light shining through the curtains, which surprised me but did not awaken me dramatically. At first I assumed I had left one of the hall lights on, but there was something about it, a flickering, a dimness, which warned me that this was not electric. It was a candle or hurricane lamp: something with a burning flame. It was a yellow, and not a white light.

The door was on the latch. Immediately I was in the hall, I could sense them. I *smelled* them, as one can smell animals. A kind of leafiness mixed with stale sweat. And scent, or perfume. No, a man's aftershave. My own cologne. I think that the woman was wearing it.

My house has a long living-room which runs the full length of the building. Its wide window makes the most of the poor northern light and gives me a broad vision of the river a mile below, when there is no foliage on the trees to blind me. In the summer a crack willow, greatly loved by jays and magpies, stretches its arms out and cuts off the river-view from me. Occasionally, I catch sight of a small white triangle, the sail of a river yacht; or a flash of silver through the greenery. But mostly I don't bother to look in the summer. I wait for the river to appear once again, through the old willow's skeleton, late in the month of November. It comes out of the rustic leaves like a backdrop of old hammered silver.

They were huddled together at the end of this long room, under the open staircase. There was an old blanket I recognised, draped over the space beneath the stairs, making a rough kind of tent. The woman was sitting in front of the tent with a jam jar that held a lit candle. One of the men was busying himself with sewing; the tall one I think, but it was difficult to tell because he was bent over his work and apparently intent on small stitches. The candlelight must have been straining his eyes. The other man was nowhere to be seen.

The woman looked up and saw me staring through the doorway, and I hurried away, embarrassed at being caught. I went into the kitchen and put on a kettle to make a cup of tea. Then I went back into the living-room, purposely averting my eyes from the camp-site, and switched on a tall standard lamp.

Light flooded into the room.

I didn't know what to do then. I didn't want to disturb them, nor they to disturb me, so I switched on the television and pulled the long sofa round, and that way I lay with my back to them, and tried to wipe thought from my brain cells.

But all through the evening, behind and before me, I was surrounded by noise of some kind. Sometimes I couldn't tell where the noise came from; American street violence from the low television, or soft sounds of housework conducted behind me. Once, I started as a shadow swept across me, but it was only the small, rounded man going for water, creeping so as not to disturb me. He filled their tin can at the sink, then made his way back to his friends. Or maybe they weren't his friends, perhaps they were relatives; or perhaps, as with me, they were strangers as he was himself. Maybe they were all strangers. Even the baby, as yet unborn, was a mystery to its mother. She didn't *know* it: not as a human being. She knew it as a human lump, an emotion, a feeling, she might kill for if it was threatened. But she didn't know it, not as Harry, nor Deborah, nor as a son, nor a daughter. It was just an extension of her.

One of the men burped as I finished my late night drink. He sounded like Malcom J. I almost turned around and frowned, but managed to hold myself back. I cannot stand makers of bodily sound: the suckers and belchers, farters and sniffers, and hawkers, they all drive me crazy. I hate public toilets where men clear their nasal passages, some men must be nothing but mucus inside. I once threw a bread roll at a man as he ate in a restaurant because he made sounds as he chewed. The man was a pig, he just sucked at his food, oblivious of all those around him. My wife was alive then. She made an apology when I wouldn't stand up and do it. She said I suffered from tinnitus and was short tempered when it came to most noises. The man had the gall to ask what he'd been doing and I could have willingly jumped up and killed him. Perhaps my wife would have lived if I'd done that. It's something that I've often thought about. Maybe there's a set number of spaces for the dead, and if I'd filled a slot for her she would not have been car-crashed. I don't know. I've thought about it. I'm sure it doesn't work retrospectively, though. You can't bring people back, only stop them from going. And I don't know if you can even do that.

At a quarter-past-ten I went out to the kitchen and washed all the dishes in the sink. There were three extra cups there, no plates and no cutlery, nothing but three china cups. I washed them along with my own bits of crockery, and left them on the surface to dry.

Then I went back to my long living-room and switched off the TV and turned all the lights down and took myself upstairs to bed. For the first time in a long time, and rather surprisingly, I fell asleep almost immediately.

And then it was Saturday, and I did very little, and I just spent my time hanging round the house.

But that night, the Saturday night, I woke up quite suddenly, and sat up in bed with a start. There was a thin beam of light sweeping slowly round the room, and a soft rustling sound from the corner, where the chest of drawers stands. I held my breath and listened. Whispers were coming from that part of the room and when I peered out from the sheets I could see shapes and lumps lying there, three bodies slumped on the floor. Then the torch flashed on my face and I slammed shut my eyelids, pretending to still be asleep. The whispering went on for quite some time after that, but nothing that I could decipher.

An hour and a half later I still couldn't drop off. The squatters hadn't fallen asleep either, I could still hear them rustling like bats in the darkness. When I looked again a shaft of moonlight which came through a crack in the curtains revealed that they'd tossed their blanket across a chair back and attached it to the chest of drawers, effectively shutting themselves off.

I switched on my bedside lamp and put the radio on.

I was in time to tune in to the shipping forecast, and it sounded a 'moderate' night. At the end of it, I was still wide awake. But the noise from behind the squatters' awning had ceased as if they had fallen asleep. There were slow breathing sounds from that corner.

Later, much later, I watched the dawn creep into the room through that same narrow crack in the curtains. I got up ragged, my head still buzzing, and made myself a strong pot of tea. When it had brewed I poured a cup, and heard a noise behind me. There was the tin can, on the draining-board beside me. I filled it, took mine back to bed.

Sunday passed much the same way.

I awoke on Monday to a shrill, broken screaming, and crawled out of a thick fog, still groggy and unable to focus. The noise was the telephone. The telephone was ringing. I managed to lift the receiver.

'Yeah? What is it?'

I listened to Malcom J Barnett's voice.

'Where are you prick-head?'

'What?' I glanced at the bedside clock, and it told me it was just after eleven. God Almighty, I must have fallen asleep again; a half-empty cup of cold tea told me that. 'I think I'm sick,' I said. 'I've been to the doctors.'

'Pull the other one, moron, don't you know what day it is? It's BF day, and that's nothing to do with *barf.* If you're really sick you'd better be on crutches, or sporting an external catheter.'

Malcolm J's second attempts at wit were always better than his first. He seemed to need a marker shot to get his brain pointing in the right direction before he could go for the bull.

'Listen...' I said, but the phone had gone dead on me. Malcolm J had no time for my sickness.

God, a staff meeting. If I didn't turn up today I wouldn't know what was going on for the rest of the month, Franklyn doesn't take time to repeat himself, and nobody else would advise me. Franklyn also takes absence from his monthly staff meeting as a personal insult to himself and his entire family; popular myth has it that contracts are taken out on those who have failed to attend twice. Faces have simply disappeared overnight. I had to get going to catch the twelve-thirty and be in the office by two, or the mysteries of the afterlife would probably be revealed to me, a lot sooner than I hoped to encounter them.

I pulled on my trousers and went into the bathroom, where my toothpaste tube had been hideously mutilated. I flattened it out, cleaned my teeth, washed, shaved and went into the bedroom and threw on the first clothes I found. One of the squatters was disturbed by my antics and poked his head out of the awning. He looked kind of quizzical, but I was still fumbling. I left him without a 'good morning'.

I caught the twelve-thirty by the barest of margins, and cursed all the way to Liverpool Street.

Franklyn was in one hell of a mood and I had to endure his admonishments and a lecture on the perils of late nights. Malcolm J Barnett stood behind him making faces, and rolling in his mud-pit of smugness. I tried to explain that I wasn't really feeling well, but Franklyn wasn't born yesterday. He could recognise a late night from fifty feet away. It was no use attempting to tell him about insomnia, Franklyn had no time for that. There *is* no insomnia, you simply lack self-discipline. One should force oneself into oblivion. I'd heard it all before. The only way you lose your sleep is by staying up all night making merry. It isn't that Franklyn is some kind of puritan, on business trips he runs you quite ragged. He takes you to brothels and night clubs and discos. He takes you where life is most seedy.

I once accompanied him on a trip to Manchester, and three days in his company practically made me demented. After the business of the day he would get drunk, he would leer (and I mean *really* leer) at any unfortunate hotel receptionist until I almost gagged with embarrassment for him, and then we'd go out on the town. I wouldn't go willingly, he always had to drag me, and at four a.m. or some time like that he'd decide to get down to some business, like tactics or strategies for the coming day's meetings. I would be taken to his room, have the portable typewriter thrust on me, and be commanded to take down the slurred battle plans which I knew would be abandoned in the morning. My eyes would be leaden and my brain humming, but I still had to take down his rambling rubbish, the signs of his drunken, mad ego.

Bernard Franklyn, bless his black heart, is certainly no kind of angel. And of course, there's the bloodless bond, the kosher screw he enjoys twice weekly. No, he doesn't expect us to be choirboys, but if you good-timed the night away, you cleaned up, put on a fresh shirt and turned up at the office looking as if you had gone to bed at nine o'clock the night before and dreamed of nothing more sordid than daffodils.

The interview ended with him blowing smoke in my face and giving me a full frontal outlook on his stained and crooked teeth.

The day rather dissipated after that. Eventually I found myself opening my front door, walked into the living room, on into the kitchen and found that my foodstuff was depleted. God, they'd only been there two days and half my food was missing. They must have stacked it up behind their blanket, and be sitting there as if they were guarding it. They must have stacked it pretty neatly to get it and three humans crammed into the corner. I hoped they'd not stolen the good stuff.

Monica called round at seven; I'd forgotten we were going to the cinema. She sat and waited while I got ready, smoking my cigarettes and staring at the blanket, and occasionally she tried to peer round it. There had been absolutely no movement from behind the tent since I had returned home from work. I was beginning to think that the squatters might have left me, and I wondered if they'd left any food behind. I wasn't truly lying when

Monica called out, 'What the hell's that blanket for?' and I replied, rather casually, 'Nothing, really, it's just hiding some foodstuff, I haven't got around to unpacking it.'

'What kind of foodstuff?' she said.

'Just some shopping. I had a big blitz on it and I haven't got room for it all. I thought I might get it in monthly, instead of in bits at a time.'

'It doesn't work like that,' she said. 'You still get the bits no matter what you've got in the cupboards.'

'I did my best,' I finished lamely, and I wished she was not so disparaging.

I heard the armchair squeak and I knew she had got up to look. Monica can be quite a nosey woman sometimes. I ran to get there before her.

'Why don't you come in here?' I said, dragging her into the bedroom.

'Why, what's going on in there?' she asked, but her expression said 'I know what for'. She gave me one of her lustful smiles, and blew cigarette smoke in my face.

'I thought I might show you something. If you play your cards right.' I had to go through with it now.

(Sometimes, to be honest, I'm not really sure that I like Monica. Sometimes I think I just feign it.)

We went into the bedroom and stripped down to our underclothes, and clambered between icy sheets. Monica moaned about it, but then she likes moaning. I wished we had gone to the pictures. It took a lot of caressing with both pairs of hands to get me anywhere near ready for her and every time the top blankets moved a woman-smell wafted up from down below. Mostly that odour gets me going, but I wasn't really in the mood, and it did nothing but put me off. Monica will keep talking, too, especially right in the middle of it. Sometimes it's love-talk like 'Oh darling, I do think you're wonderful, I do love you, do you love me? You don't have to say you do just because I'm asking, oh but I love you anyway.' At other times it's mere chatter, as if we were standing at a bus stop. Monica feels threatened by silence, especially when we're making love. I simply grunt out non-committal noises. Monica does not seem to mind that.

And she has always got there first. She doesn't know it, but it's now become a race, which I must always lose. I'll never win it, *because* it has become a race. There's no bigger turn-off than having something on your mind when you're trying to get something from your loins. So, she always gets there first and, I suspect, always will. I'm destined to lose because I'm so anxious about winning the race I can't relax enough to immerse myself into the joy of sex. I get too worked up beforehand, doing mental warm-up exercises, sexual fantasy limberings and stretching exercises for my libido; by the time the race starts my psychological tendons are already so taut I'm liable to snap a hamstring before entry. So Monica gets there first, and I get there second, and I suspect one day, I won't even make it at all.

Then after she's come, while I'm doggedly working towards my climax, thinking, 'come on, for Christ's sake man, COME ON,' and trying to concentrate on the silky feel of her body, she *encourages* me with more talk. 'You're nearly there. Do you want me to talk dirty? Fucky Monica, come on darling *nearly* there, fucky, fucky, can you feel me gripping you with my honey-pot? Ooouu you make my nipples tingle.' Stuff like that really puts me off, and one day I am going to destroy our relationship by screaming, 'SHUT UP YOU STUPID WOMAN I'M TRYING TO CONCENTRATE!' Then when I *finally* make it and am enjoying those brief few seconds as my passion zithers out of me and into her, her own passion is so far in the past she gives a sort of giggle and cuddles me as if to say 'well done', which I HATE, because I'm not a little boy who's just done his first pee-pee into a potty. When SHE gets there, it's as if she's seen GOD in person. 'OHHHHHH OOOOOOH GUGUGUGKRYYYST!!!' And I stay quiet, letting her enjoy those intense moments when the tidal waves come, one after another, and the last thing anyone wants to hear is a GIGGLE.

I never used to have any trouble reaching a climax when I made love with my wife. We rarely made it *together* but sometimes it was me and sometimes her first. I didn't even have to think about it. I just came. But I suppose you get used to one partner and when you get another one the rhythms are all wrong and things don't happen at the right times and the build-up fails somewhere. I used to think it was because Monica was too big, or I was too small, or something like that, but I'm sure it was simply because our sexual couplings were unusual to my body, and irregular.

Tonight, neither of us even saw the finish line. It was a false start. Shortly after we left the blocks and I was proceeding at a leisurely pace, worrying as usual about the sprint down the final hurdle, Monica stiffened in my arms.

'What on earth's that noise?' she said.

'What noise?' I muttered.

'Listen. Listen. In the other room.'

It's the cat,' I muttered.

She moved beneath me.

'You haven't got a cat.'

No I haven't. That was a poor thing to say. 'I got one at the weekend,' I said, thinking that now I would either have to get a cat, or lose one very quickly. Then I remembered the neighbours, the Saunders, and I dragged them into my strange deception. 'It belongs to the neighbours. You remember, I looked after it for them last year, while they were away on holiday.'

She relaxed a bit, but said, 'It's November. Where have they gone in November?'

'To Thailand.'

'Oh,' she said, and then we'd kind of run out of love-making, so we got up and went to the pictures.

I wondered what made me lie so devoutly, as if I had something to hide. Why didn't I just come out and mention the squatters? It was because I was afraid she'd confront them. Monica is good at confronting people. She does it with practised abandon, in shops and in restaurants, '...this blouse has a mark on it. I don't expect blouses with marks on them. You take off some money or take back the goods. I know the Sale of Goods Act inside out young lady.' She's good at things like that. 'This chicken's underdone. I don't want to have to report this place, but you should know about salmonella. You can get salmonella from undercooked meat...' Car park attendants walk in fear of Monica. She destroys public servants by trainloads. She has no heart when it comes to incompetence, mistakes, neglect, or human failing. She goes in and then she confronts it. Monica calls it 'being assertive'; but I have another name for it. I think it's the kind of thing that you see in concentration camps, and places where people do things to other people that later are regretted on a national scale. She's fond of saying, 'I don't suffer fools gladly,' which does nothing but infuriate me. The inference is that the speaker is someone who has never done one foolish thing in their life. There's inherent condescension, a sense of superiority which goes with that casual remark. And, frankly, it makes me want to throw up.

I think I was dozing through most of the picture, but Monica didn't appear to observe it.

I thank the Lord for these small mercies. I hope that I don't have to pay for them.

DOG PEOPLE: FOUR

Another Saturday came and I really had to get out of the house. The squatters had got hold of a radio from somewhere (perhaps it was one of my old ones) and had tuned it to one of the pirate stations. I'm not one for 'background,' I like weekends peaceful, so I went out in my old Colt Estate. It's actually a 'Sigma', which my garage man calls 'Stigma' no matter how many times I correct him. I drove far out into the marshes.

There was a hard white crust upon the reeds, as if salt had been spread across the land and had then mixed with water and congealed. I suppose it was nothing but frost. Normally the marshes are damp, a kind of eternal dampness that would make one's life hell if you actually had to exist in it; but, in winter, the wetness is frozen. There *are* houses out there: ramshackle weatherboarded places existing on stilts, green-black slime creeps out of the mud, making the stilts look gangrenous, and the roofs look as if they might become a source of fossil fuels for distant generations of Essexians.

A grey heron rose into an opalescent sky, and I thought of how much I despise them. The stagnant pool within my woods had once been a thriving community, full of fish and darting frogs, and newts and waterboatmen. But a heron I could never thwart kept pillaging it of that life, in the early hours of every morning, on raids like a senseless barbarian. You can't shoot herons: they are a protected species. And somehow they seem to know that. They appear to be aware that they are above the law, that they can do anything with impunity. They are like Japanese emperors, or embassy staff protected by diplomatic immunity. If they had the ounce, herons could rob the wealthy aristocrats and landowners of their expensive koi carp and the gentry could not demand recompense. But herons are too stupid for that; they stick to petty burglary, coming out of the dawn and stealing from the poor. Herons are the small-minded habitual criminals which creep through the ranks of the bird world.

Along the dyke which keeps the sea from flooding the marshes, I could see several keen ornithologists. They come out here in the winter to see the Brent geese which fly down from Iceland whenever that's a bad winter up there; as many as two-hundred thousand of them. There are also knots and sandpipers and oyster catchers, stalking about in the mud. The tide goes out for nearly two miles, and the birds peck away after shellfish. Oystercatchers don't actually eat oysters, they eat mainly ragworm and lugworm; but 'lugworm catchers' is somewhat prosaic, and I guess some birds deserve some small romance.

I got out of the car and took a walk along the top of the dyke. The wind was cutting across the mud and it was bitterly cold. In the middle of the marshes, up against the sea wall, is a testing area for field guns owned by the Ministry of Defence. You can stroll alongside it when there's no red warning flag flying. Out on this piece of land are huge blocks of concrete and sheets of metal which have been brutally punched full of holes. It's an eerie place, a Ballardian landscape (if you happen to be familiar with that writer's books), and one is likely to come across mangled pieces of metal that once were immaculate gunshells.

As I was examining a piece of punctured rusty metal, I saw a group of six or seven people, huddled around something on the ground. A spaniel was sniffing at their legs, then running away and back again, as if it were impatient to be out on the mud.

When I reached this group, neatly togged out in waxed jackets and green wellingtons, I saw that there was an elderly man on the ground. Someone had put a coat under his head, to act as a rough kind of pillow. His face was grey and dotted with sweat, and his eyes protruded with a frightened look and I recognised him as a man I saw catching the train sometimes, when I was going to work.

'Someone's gone for an ambulance,' whispered a woman who had mysteriously placed herself next to me.

'Does anyone know him?' asked a man, who seemed to be taking charge of the problem.

'I do,' I said. But then I amended it. 'No, I'm afraid I don't, really.'

'Well which is it?' the man asked briskly. 'Yes or no? It can't be both.'

'He catches my train,' I replied, 'sometimes. But I'm afraid I don't know his name.'

'Well that's a lot of good, then,' muttered the chief of operations, as if it were a personal insult to him that I did not possess the knowledge he required in order to make himself complete master of the situation. He was probably bossed around by his wife and his kids back home.

'Why don't you look in his wallet?' I said, and a disapproving stare from the chief of operations told me that this kind of thing wasn't done, old chap, we're British and civilised here. 'Well how the hell else are you going to find out?' I said, irked by his foolish affliction. 'What's the matter with him, anyway? Has he had some kind of heart attack?'

And the woman next to me was appalled. 'You don't say that kind of thing,' she muttered. 'It's not good for him, to hear things like that.'

'He must know he's lying there for something. You're not just relaxing, are you?' I said to the man on the ground.

He stared back with terrified eyes.

'Of course he's not relaxing!' the woman said angrily. 'And I think you should show more consideration.'

Maybe she was right.

The sound of a siren drifted over the marshes, and all of our heads turned in unison.

'Ambulance is on its way,' said the chief, to what looked like a heart attack victim, and he gave him a reassuring pat.

But a moment later we saw two policemen making their way along the top of the dyke. They were talking into their collars. When they reached us, one of them said, 'What's the trouble. Is somebody ill?'

'No,' I said. 'He's just relaxing.'

The policeman glared at me and motioned with his eyes to his partner. I was clearly not wanted, and maybe I deserved it, so I turned away and left them all to it. They were calling for ambulances into their collars, and getting hisses and crackles for replies. The chief of operations was in deep conversation with the smaller of the two policemen, and the woman was smiling at the other, as if now, no one could possibly die of heart failure. Not now the law had arrived.

She caught up with me as I went down into the marshes. She was big, middle-class and county. I was in for a ticking off from an aunt or mother-in-law who scared the hell out of relations. The smell of damp tweed hit my nostrils.

'I think that was a quite disgraceful way to behave,' she said. 'You ought to be thoroughly ashamed of yourself. That man was quite obviously ill.'

'Oh God, lady,' I said. 'Spare me your lectures, I didn't mean to hurt the old man. It just seems so ridiculous, standing around like that. We might as well try to be natural. I don't see the point in concealing the obvious, he must have known what was happening as well as the rest of us.'

The woman gave me a glare like thunder.

'I suppose you think it's clever, that kind of talk? It's time someone gave you a piece of their mind.'

'If I'm that clever I don't need bits of other people's brains, especially not yours, which is pickled in meaningless phrases.'

'You're a damned hooligan!' she shouted.

'Lady, I'm thirty-seven years of age, so go home and frighten your grandchildren.' I don't know why I was picking on this woman, but all of my life superior people have been telling me what I should do. They've been sneering at certain holes in my education, taking exceptions to some of my reactions. I think that, on that day, it all caught up with me, and I had to let off steam at someone. I can't understand why these circumstances demand such behaviour. You see a man on the ground, obviously ill, and you're supposed to talk in sepulchral voices as if he was already dead. And, more importantly, you're supposed to *care* about him. I have to be honest: it did not really matter to me whether the man lived or died. I would prefer him to live because even the death of a stranger touches my own mortality. And I would not deliberately let a man die if I could help him in any way. In this case an ambulance had already been called for, and there was very little else we could do.

I got down on my knees in the cold, frosty grass because the woman was still there, glaring at me. I had to do something. She was burning me with her righteous indignation, her holy wrath.

'Let us pray that this man lives,' I said to the fuming matron before me. 'Let us ask God to unblock his arteries and stop his heart from bursting.' She gave a gasp of horror and retreated a couple of paces. 'I can't promise it will work, though,' I said, 'because I tried it when my wife and child died. It doesn't often work, unless the victim's name is Lazarus, and then there are no guarantees. I should have called my own son 'Lazarus' and maybe it would have worked then. Or my wife should have been called 'Mrs Lazarus'. But we'll give it a try, anyway. What do you think, do you want to join me?' I smiled as my hands clasped together.

'You're mad!' said the woman, escaping to sanity with the muttering of two holy words.

'Mad? I'm mad? Mad for praying? In that case my vicar's a lunatic, and the bishop, and all of his clergy. They pray for sick people all the time, every Sunday, or didn't you know about that?'

She turned in her brogues and began to run, scurrying back to the policemen. I got to my feet and retreated myself. I didn't want any stress from the policemen, who would side with the old county dame; particularly since I had already blotted my copy book.

When I got home, still engrossed in that moment, there was a dead rabbit lying on the draining board. It had a snare around its neck and was oozing blood down the stainless steel channels of the drainer. I wondered if it was a gift from the squatters, or whether I had interrupted them and they had just left it there, intending to return to it later. I glanced through the door and into the living-room. All three of them were there, crouched in a circle eating cold beans from a can they had filched from my cupboard.

I think that the rabbit was a gift. I think. But I may never know that for certain.

The telephone rang.

I picked it up and said 'Hello?'

'Who was that, a minute ago?' It was Monica, with one of her fluttering phone calls.

'What are you talking about? I just got in.' It was hard to concentrate, I couldn't take my eyes off the rabbit. Its own glazed orbs seemed locked to my own. I could hear the slow drip of its blood in the sink. (I happen to be a vegetarian.)

'I rang a few minutes ago. A strange woman answered.'

'On this phone? I only just got in.'

'You already said that,' said Monica. 'Is anyone else there? I don't mind, just so long as you tell me. I mean, it could be your mother for all I know. It could be a visiting cousin.'

Oh God, Monica, I thought. 'There's nobody else here. What did she say?' I had turned until I was looking at the pregnant woman in the living-room, and suddenly I was very curious. 'What kind of woman did she sound like?' I asked.

'She sounded a lot like Pamela, but it wasn't. And anyway, it doesn't really matter. You know I'm not the jealous type.' But she sounded kind of jealous to me.

'It wasn't Pamela. Pamela's not here,' I said.

'I know,' replied Monica. 'It's just that it sounded like her. You know how she speaks, rather plummy. Anyway, I don't think Pamela would say, *Tell him the rabbit's for the dog.'*

I looked at the corpse on the bloody-red drainer, how could she see down the telephone? Then I realised, Monica was telling me what the woman had said.

'That's something of a peculiar thing to come out with,' I said. 'Are you sure she was talking to you? Maybe you got a crossed line or something. I think you must have had a crossed line.'

'I don't think so. I might have thought so, except for your clock in the background.'

What clock? Then I remembered, I have a chiming clock on the mantelpiece, a Napoleon's hat set in rosewood. It chimes every hour and again on the half-hour. Trust Monica to phone when the clock chimed.

It didn't seem worth making a meal out of the issue, so I decided it was best to say nothing. If she saw the blood dripping I'm sure she'd know why; but then, Monica doesn't always see things like that.

Monica read more into my silence than I was intending. 'You're sure you haven't got Pamela there?' she asked me.

'Yes, I'm sure. It wasn't Pamela. There's nobody here except me.'

'That's okay,' she said, rather quietly. 'Don't forget we have a date for this evening. I'll pick you up round about eight.'

'Yes, okay,' I said. 'I'll see you a bit later. Be careful, the roads might be icy.'

'All right,' she said, and then she hung up on a glum note.

I replaced my own receiver and spent a long time gloomily staring at the rabbit. I didn't want to have to touch it, but I didn't know how long it might remain lying there. Perhaps if I simply left it one of the squatters would come and remove all the carnage. I wondered if now the man on the sea wall looked that way, if that's how he looked at this moment. He had run into an invisible snare, out there in the marshes and was possibly lying on some kind of draining board, oozing his bodily fluids.

But if I left it there, and they *didn't* remove it, the corpse would go rotten and maggoty. I remembered a Roman Polanski film, where a rabbit heaved with bluebottle larvae. The thought was enough to make me ill.

'I haven't got a dog,' I said, addressing the living-room doorway. But the squatters appeared to take no notice. The empty bean can was lying crushed, on the carpet. The tall bearded man was leaning back on his hands, his face skyward and his eyes closed, as if he were some kind of hedonist relaxing in sunshine. The smaller one was stretched out lengthways with his head in the lap of the woman, and her bulge overshadowed him. She stared away into the dark middle distance.

Did they *want* me to get a dog? I wondered. I don't suppose I'd mind, just so long as they looked after it. I would have to think about that one, when I had some time left for thinking.

The bearded man lifted an arm and without opening his eyes, scratched at a sore on his cheek. It looked like ringworm to me. He ought to be careful. I turned away, rather concerned for him.

I went back into the kitchen, took a carving knife from a drawer and used it to lift the rabbit onto a plastic bag. Then, retching a little and squirming away from the scent of death's rapid corruption, I carried it outside and hurled the lot skywards. The foxes would deal with it later.

Unable to settle after that I drove the car down to the chemist shop in the village and bought some Mycota cream. Ringworm is a fungus, I knew that much, and this was the ointment to deal with it. I had had ringworm, myself, as a kid, I knew exactly how irritating it could be. I took the medication back to the house and left it on the carpet, by the squatters.

And then the phone rang again.

'What did you tell her that for?' a voice asked.

'Who is this?' I said.

'It's Pamela, you know that. And you told Monica that I was round at your house.'

'No, I didn't,' I said. 'It was a misunderstanding. Pamela, it was just some kind of joke.'

'I didn't find it funny,' she told me. 'And if it had been true, I wouldn't have minded. But you've never even invited me there.'

'I'm sorry,' I apologised. 'It was a misunderstanding. Who gave you my number anyway? Monica? She knows I was only messing around. This is her way of getting back at me, because she wouldn't admit she had a crossed line, and she thought someone sounded like you. I'm sorry, Pamela, I'll...' but the phone had gone dead on me, like the rabbit, and possibly the man on the sea wall. The trouble was, Monica knew very well that Pamela being there was one of my fantasies, even if I did try to make a joke of it on some occasions. She knew that I sometimes changed her face for Pamela's, while we were making love. Women know these things. They can also mind-read. Monica would turn and look at me sometimes, when I was thinking of something I wanted to keep from her, and her look told me that she *knew* what I was thinking, and there was nothing I could do to conceal it. Sometimes, when we're lying side by side and I'm supposed to be asleep but the cogs are turning ten to the dozen and I'm trying to decide whether to be unfaithful to Monica and try for Pamela, Monica will say, suddenly, 'What are you thinking about?' her words coming out of the darkness like gunshots.

'Nothing,' I will say. 'I'm trying to get to sleep.'

'Like hell,' she retorts. 'I can hear the wheels and levers moving in there. If you don't want to tell me, that's okay.'

'There's nothing to tell.' I become exasperated. 'I really just want to get to sleep. How can I sleep while you're psycho-analysing me?'

'Suit yourself.'

But she *knows,* you see. And that makes me even more awkward.

Why can't I do something on my own? Why can't I surprise people with an action they haven't been expecting? Am I the freak, the only one in the world without this gift of prediction? Does everyone but me know what everyone else is going to do next? How can I plan anything if they all know what I intend to do and treat me like a child who has sent notes on ahead, saying, 'I need to fuck Pamela at least once before I die. I want to hold her hand and whisper secrets.'

She wants me too, and I know because she loves like a puff ball exploding, in every direction. She wouldn't mind it being with me. She wouldn't mind it being with Michael Douglas, but she wouldn't mind it being me either. Pamela's like that.

Oh hell. I gave in. You can't defeat mind-readers. I gave up and mopped up the bloodstains. I wonder if there's such a thing as mental stigmata? I wonder about all kinds of things these days.

DOG PEOPLE: FIVE

At the end of November, when the leaves were like brittle glass under my feet, I had a terrible urge. I had a sudden irrational desire to visit the place where my family was killed. I never ignore irrational urges: they come from somewhere deep inside and it is much more important to take notice of these than of any sensible reasonable desires. The conscious part of the brain is a puny instrument: the subconscious has all the power. All the symbols and images have been stored there since men carried clubs and had to go out and whack their meals to death before they could eat. Man was much closer to life and death then. He carried the sun, earth and moon in his head.

Never mind that it was the middle of the night. That's the best time to undertake absurd subliminally-activated treks. I got into the Colt and drove through the deserted streets to the A127.

I often passed the stump that was all that was left of the killer tree, but I always looked the other way when I drove that stretch of road. It hurt me to see it. At the time of the accident I nearly went crazy trying to figure out whether it was the car that killed them, or the tree itself. Was it the invincible force or the immovable object? If they had not been in the car, on a course for the tree, perhaps they would never have died. If the tree had not been there, they would never have died. If *I'd* driven, they might not have died.

And it was such a *solid* tree. It must have been thirty years old, at least, a sycamore with an armspan girth. If it had been *three* years old, if the people who had planted it had waited a few years before lining the arterial road with sycamores, then my wife may not have been destroyed that day. The tree would have snapped in two, the car would have gone through a three-strand wire fence and come to rest in a frost-hard field beyond. Was it too much to ask them to wait a few years before performing their good civic duty? Who needs trees along dual carriageways like the Southend arterial anyway? They just get covered in oil and dirt and make the verge look even drabber than ever.

So, was it the tree's fault? Or the man who planted it? He was probably still alive somewhere, enjoying his children, or even grandchildren; he still had his family to give gifts to at Christmas. He still had someone who called out as he entered, 'Is that you, dear? How was your day at work? I've booked us up for the theatre this Saturday. Mum's going to look after the baby.'

Or maybe, more likely, the car was to blame. It was a mangled mess after the accident, all torn metal, punctured, like those sheets out on the field gun testing site. The upholstery had been ripped apart, as if by a maniac with a knife. Bloodstains over everything. Was it the car? Faulty steering? Faulty brakes? Faulty fucking hub caps? What?

Should the victim's husband have painstakingly investigated every aspect, every square inch of the wreck, for something wrong, something to finger the blame? What if he *had* done? What if he found a tiny screw inside the brake disc, dropped by mistake by some careless mechanic? What if, at the last service, they hadn't bothered to change the brake linings at all, had said, what the hell, we'll leave it till next time, he won't know the difference, just charge him. They've got a good three thou on those linings...? What would *he* have done? Waited outside some night club for the mechanic, unrecognisable out of his oily overalls and slicked up for Saturday night, waited with a hammer to spill out his brains on the pavement in front of a screaming girlfriend? Would that have stopped the nightmares, and made him feel better?

'Oh God yes, it would!' I gave vent to my futility as the headlamps swept the blackness away from the road ahead. I realised I was crying. I also realised I had been thinking of myself in the third person. That man, whose wife and son had been killed, that man wasn't me. It was somebody else. It had to be, or I would go mad.

'Anyway,' I muttered savagely, 'at least the tree died too!'

It gave me some satisfaction to say that.

When I got to the spot where the accident happened, I steered the car onto the verge. It was a desolate place. The whole length of the A127 is desolate, except where it's built up, and there the houses look desolate too.

I left the headlights on and went to the stump, stripped clean of its bark now, and white under the starlight. A dirty white. I ran my hand over the jagged toothlike top.

'Murdering bastard,' I said.

A car went past and I watched as it sped along the road. Its lights illuminated other trees, other stumps.

Other stumps?

I stood there for a long while, hunched into my overcoat, watching as cars went past. There *were* other stumps. I could see at least two of them. What if I'd got the wrong one? Was I accusing the wrong stump of killing my wife and child? Perhaps this stump was responsible for the death of someone else's wife? Were they all tombstumps? Or maybe some of the trees had been brought down by a wind? Why was it all so damn complicated? I should have marked the stump after the accident, cut the words KILLER TREE on what was left of the trunk. Now I would never know which one it was. I had lost the spot where I had lost my family. Damn. And, for good measure, *Damn*!

Maybe I should go back to my old practice of mutilating Escort 1.3 LX's, running keys down their paintwork, breaking their radio aerials, murmuring softly, 'Take that you bastard, and there's a lot more to come yet,' and kicking dents into the door panel, if I could get away with making some noise.

God, it was futile. I drove home to bed. The squatters were asleep on the living-room floor and I tiptoed between them, careful not to wake them, and I locked myself inside my bedroom.

'What do you mean by coming into work wearing trainers?'

Franklyn looked more amazed than angry, as if I had just performed some conjuring trick he had never seen attempted before. I looked down at my feet. The fact was, the smaller of the two squatters had helped himself to my work shoes, and had put them inside their tent in the living-room, and I couldn't find one of the others. So I was wearing trainers.

'I'm sorry. I'll go out and get a proper pair. I've put the wrong ones on.'

'You've been sitting there wearing them for the last two hours. Didn't you notice?'

'No,' I said.

Franklyn made an impatient gesture with his hand. 'Go on. Get out and get a decent pair of shoes.'

I stood there.

His eyebrows lifted. 'Well?'

'The fact is, I've run out of money. My card is up to the hilt, and....I just haven't got any money.'

We remained motionless for a moment, like two gunfighters, each waiting for the other to make a move. I could sense Malcolm J hovering on the sidelines, blinking away like an owl. He was crapping himself. Malcolm J likes his waters unruffled, and although this wasn't him who was getting the flak, he couldn't believe anyone could be so moronic as to come to work wearing their trainers. This kind of thing rocks his faith in the stability of the universe. You couldn't talk to Malcolm J about the Big Bang theory, or the formation of planets from gases. The earth was a solid lump of rock which had always been there and always would be; the sun was something which tanned your skin in Spain and the stars were twinkly spots occasionally seen as you staggered home late from a party. People who did unpredictable things were mad people who interfered with the order of things, who knocked links out of the chain of being, who deserved to be hung, or at least to be sacked. But what worried him most of all was the thought that one day he might actually do this himself, in a brainstorm; he might go and do something crazy. Malcolm J's nightmares were of the kind where he found himself dressed only in a short vest in the middle of a supermarket while shoppers passed him by and sniggered as he tried to cover his genitals with a can of pink salmon.

'You want *me* to loan you the money?' cried Franklyn at last.

'Well, no,' I said. 'I wasn't meaning that. It was just that....'

'BARNETT,' roared Franklyn.

'Yes, sir?' He came skidding up alongside me.

'Barnett, can you lend your – your friend here the money to get himself a new pair of shoes?'

Malcolm J said, 'He's not – yessir, I think so. That is, no cash, but I've got my cheque-book – '

'Then take him out and buy him some footwear.'

'Yes sir.'

Exit Franklyn, his great wrath subsiding. He'd probably have a good laugh about it, with the mistress. '...and then the little prat has the nerve, he says to me – not there, a bit higher, that's better – he has the, ha, ha, the nerve to say that he didn't know he was wearing the things. I ask you – steady, steady, not too hard – no, harder than that – he has the nerve, I mean could *you* travel over an hour to work and not notice you're wearing your – what? you? no, never, don't tell me things like that – and *then* he says, bold as brass! how about lending me twenty quid to go and get a new pair of shoes? – I said, no, I'm *not* kidding, the little prick asked me for it, I said – what? – what do you take me for? I gave him to Barnett. Let that tub of lard sub him – got to admit, though, he's got to have some kind of bottle, eh? He's got to have some kind of bottle.'

Malcolm J Barnett would have nightmares for two weeks to come.

I was exhausted when I got home that night. The squatters had made a can of tea and, without asking, I took some myself. It didn't taste quite the same as my own tea, I think they were still using pond-water, but old habits die hard.

I had to think about my finances, because I walk a knife-edge at the best of times. Now I had squatters who had moved in with me, and I had to buy their food as well. If I wasn't careful, I'd get into debt. They were also using my gas and electricity, and little things like soap and the towels. These things can mount up, it's the little things which kill you; but there's no way that they could contribute, they looked like they were practically destitute. I had to make plans on my own.

It wasn't easy, I would like to have talked to them, but they were concealed behind their awning. I didn't want to drag them out to talk about how hard up *I* was. They had enough problems of their own.

That woman was really heavily pregnant, she shouldn't have been crawling round the floor. It can't have been comfortable, sleeping on the carpet. I wondered if, maybe, I should let her have my bed, and I could curl up in one of the armchairs. I didn't like to ask her about it though because I was, well, to tell you the truth I was shy about talking to them, I didn't think we had much in common. And I didn't want to sound condescending when I talked to her. I thought they should make the first move.

I have to say this, they were very tidy really, and they didn't overly intrude on my life. They had made a kind of permanent shelter now, in the living-room under the staircase and, really, they didn't bother me too much, we merely lived our own lives – 'together'. I think – sometimes I used to catch them watching me, and I think they wondered what I was up to, as if they were looking to me for a lead.

And I didn't really know what I should do for them; I've never had squatters before.

I noticed that they'd rearranged some of the furniture, but I think this was to make their passage a little easier because they tended to creep around the floor. There are foxes about here and they make trails through the pastures, and this was almost what the squatters were doing. In a sense, they were making their own little territory, and it encompassed about half of my living-room. I noticed that I'd stopped actually going into their half, but this was just normal politeness because they didn't often venture into mine. Once or twice they washed the dishes, but usually I did the housework.

After the tea which I'd taken from the squatters I soaked in a very long bath. I thought about a girlfriend I had once had, when I was a great deal younger. MM was a tough little tiger, always beating up other girls, and she came from a very tough family. She had four brothers who scared the lights out of me (and that's a butcher's lights). I didn't fancy her at all, I wanted to go out with a nice quiet girl called Susie, who had golden ringlets and wore dresses with frills, but MM told me I was going out with her, and her brothers could not be ignored. I went out with MM because I sincerely believed that a broken arm could be quite painful. And to make matters worse at least two of the brothers warned me that if I even 'touched her' I might as well go and order a coffin the same day.

So, I would get my arms broken if I didn't go out with her, and my neck broken if I tried anything and, all in all, it was a very fraught affair. Mahara McNiece (her father named her after a waterhole in the Arabian Desert) would violently grab me after a night at the pictures, take me into a gloomy back alley and shove me against a wall where she could grind her strong thighs against my startled and petrified groin.

'I want you,' she'd groan, with her breath like a steam-bath. 'Why don't you take my knickers down *now?*'

Mahara had a sharp face, not uncomely but hard-looking, and a lithe very muscular body. She was certainly not unattractive in a sexual sense, and she could feel my reaction (petrified but not unwilling) swelling uncertainly beneath her.

But the faces of her four brothers loomed over her shoulder on these occasions, like the giant granite faces of the American presidents at Mount Rushmore and I would find myself saying, 'Look MM, can't we wait a little while?' I used to wish I was a girl on those occasions, so that I could say it was my time of the month.

'Wait?' she would hiss, and clamping one of my hands over one of her small sharp breasts would say, 'what the hell do you want to wait for?'

'Till we're married?' I'd say.

'Don't be a prat, I'm not marrying *you*. Let's get your trousers off ...' and she'd start fumbling with my belt while inside I was screaming, *'I don't want a broken neck. I'm too young to die. Oh God, I want her. Oh God, my whole body's exploding.'*

I once asked Mahara why her daddy had named her after a waterhole in the desert. I thought, maybe he had a romantic episode there? Maybe Mahara McNiece was conceived in the mud at the edge of a pool, in a desperate struggling passion of flailing limbs and bodies? (If MM's mother took after her daughter, such a scene was not hard to imagine.) Or perhaps the waterhole had saved his life, after he had crawled over the hot sands, the victim of a plane crash or somesuch?

MM looked at me with narrowed eyes.

'If you ever mention my name again I'll kill you,' she said. 'I *hate* my name.'

And so I never did. I just lived with the fear that one of her brothers would find out I was bonking her in mysterious alleys, or (God forbid, suicide would be the easiest way out) that one day she should become pregnant.

In those far off hazy times of my youth, I used to watch Susie of the golden hair, tripping femininely down the road while MM clung like a possessive orang-utang to my arm, frequently bruising it.

'Susie,' I sighed, swilling the bathwater round my naked body, 'where are you now?' Where was MM for that matter? The last I heard of her she was dragging a Marine Commando around by his tattooed wrist, showing him off to her wimpish ex-boyfriends. The soldier, God bless him, tough as he looked, was no match for MM in her prime. I remember feeling sorry for him.

And while I was lost in this complacent reverie, I looked down and saw something crawl into my left armpit; a spider the size of a man's fist.

I leaped out of the bath with a scream, grabbed a towel and swatted myself several times, before I realised that what I had seen was my underarm hair floating on the water.

The squatters came running and peered through the doorway, as I stood dripping onto the floor, trying to wipe myself. The woman had big wet round eyes.

'I'm sorry,' I said. 'I thought I saw something.'

They stared for a few moments longer, then wandered away, into some other region of the house.

DOG PEOPLE: SIX

I had another argument today. I don't know why I get into these things, I never used to be the argumentative type, but now I'm exploding at everyone I meet, I almost go out of my way for them.

I used to be quite the opposite, in fact, I rarely had a cross word with anyone. I always rather let it roll, and saved up resentment for later. Angela used to say I was one of those husbands some women hate, because I avoided arguments and everything got bottled up. Some women (she told me) like a good blow up when the pressure starts to build. They find it relieves tensions and afterwards (apparently) you could go to bed and everything would be back to normal. I was one of those husbands that some women stab to death in their forties and everyone says, 'He was such a nice *quiet* man. I wonder what made her do it?' When Angela started to shout I would leave the house and go for a walk, commune with nature. She told me that was a despicable way to behave and that the frustration I left her with was unbelievable.

I wasn't a good husband. I never did let her have her way and fight with her. I wish now I had shouted back at her. I wish now we had had some flaming rows.

But these days, I don't know what it is. I think it might be the anniversary. I really wish to Christ I had marked that tree on the A127. It was about the last thing I had I could really despise with intensity, and now I don't even have that, because I might be mistaken. You'd think you would recognise something like that, but even a tree-stump can alter.

I suppose the anniversary also coincided with the squatters, so maybe that had something to do with it. But I don't mind the squatters, they don't worry me. In fact I think they are good for me. They stop me being so self-centred and self-pitying. It's everything else that surrounds me that gets me down.

Today I was at the shops starting to stock up with food for the squatters because I don't think they're looking after themselves properly, and I'm particularly concerned about the woman. There's a supermarket and a couple of smaller shops, and I went along to collect a few groceries. I parked outside and as I was getting out of the car I saw the man who collapsed on the sea wall. This came as a shock to me, I thought he'd be dead now, or at least on his back in a hospital bed.

But he wasn't, he was standing like a dog outside the supermarket, as if he'd been tethered to a rail while he waited. He is quite a tall man, and is going bald on top, and what hair he has left is quite silver. It looked like the frost on that day on the sea wall, and he seemed to be shivering under it. He had on a raincoat with a scarf round his neck, and was standing like some kind of zombie. He seemed to be staring at something in the distance: one of those stares that told you he was seeing a different world from everyone else. A placid, rather vacant kind of place.

I went up to him and said, 'You okay, mate?' and he turned to me and looked straight through my face. And then I realised, the man hadn't had a heart attack, he had had an attack on his senses. For some murky reason his brain had packed up on him, and he'd lain down by the river to – I don't know. Maybe he wanted to die by the river. Maybe he just didn't want to get up again. But what I was looking at were two empty eyes, and it was more chilling than if he had died.

I had the feeling that this old man wouldn't be getting on the London train any more. I once saw a dog that looked that way, and it had died about three seconds earlier. Somehow the eyes hadn't captured the message and they simply kept on staring, at nothing.

What must have happened, his wife must have taken him out for a trip, and she'd taken him down to the supermarket. She'd wrapped him up warm, and she probably walked him there slowly, and she probably held his hand tight in her own hand. When she got there, there was nothing she could do but to leave him at the door like a baby. And that's how he stood there. And he was rigidly waiting, God knows what he thought of it, and he couldn't even move until she told him.

Hell's bells, I thought. *I never want to go out that way. I never want to go out looking like a baby.*

I licked my lips, because the situation was awkward, and I gently put my hand on his elbow.

'Are you all right, mate? Do you want to go somewhere? Do you want to go down to the pub for a pint or something?'

God, I couldn't bear it, the look that he gave me, it was full of such desperate pleading.

'Can't you talk mate? Did it take all your speech away? You don't want to stand here just waiting.' It seemed so important to me, and I don't really know why, that he did something to prove he was *mortal.* If he merely stood there – he could spend his whole life there – he could give himself over to his wife. He had to do something, he had to get moving, I didn't want to see the man simply *die* there.

'Listen,' I said. '*The Victory's* not far away, I could take you down there in the car. Would you like that? We could go there and have a few glasses. What do you think? It's freezing here, you don't want to be out in it, you don't want to let it go yet.' I prayed he would do something, I prayed he would answer me. I was afraid he'd just fade like a mirage.

'It would make me happy if you'd come, it really would,' I said. 'I'd really like it. We could get drunk and - start looking at women!' I laughed, to encourage him, but he just kept on staring. He really looked as though he was quite empty.

'Come on,' I said, and I moved towards the car and, with my hand on his elbow, he followed me. I cannot describe how pitiful his steps were, but a slow thaw could have easily outpaced him.

I got the passenger door open and tried to help him into the compartment. But it wasn't easy, the man moved like erosion, it was an age before his head started lowering.

I was just about to ease him inside when a hysterical shriek hit my eardrums. 'What are you doing to my husband?' I turned around, and I couldn't believe it. His wife was tearing towards me, a short beetle-woman with stout beetle-legs, and a camel beetle-coat around her torso. God she moved fast, she could outrun a whippet; she was on me before I could straighten. 'What do you think you're doing?' she yelled at me, and she started hitting me with a bag of potatoes. 'That's my husband! What are you doing to him?'

I said, 'I'm not doing anything to him! Stop that...' I had to let go of the man to defend myself, and I ripped the potato bag out of her hands and threw it to the ground. 'I'm only trying to help your husband,' I said. 'The man is not happy, look what you're doing to him. I'm going to take him down to *The Victory* for a pint.'

'Get your hands off him. Who are you? I'm going to call a policeman.' Her lips were thin tight lines as her eyes swept the street, looking for the law.

'I know him! I was there when it happened!' I said. 'I know all the things he's afraid of.'

'You don't know anything,' she muttered, shoving past me. 'Just leave him alone. He's not well. He's all right.'

The contradictions made me even angrier for some reason.

'No he damn well isn't,' I said. 'People like you are abusing him. You're turning him into a zombie, he doesn't want to die like a baby! Nobody wants that.'

'He's not going to die!' she said, her face was both purple and white with her anger. She had a fat face like my grandmother, and my grandmother's glasses and my grandmother's grey hair.

'Let me help him,' I said, 'I can help him.' We practically wrestled over him, and the poor man swayed round like a bean-pole. Then she kicked me, and somebody else joined in, and people started coming out of the supermarket. 'Why don't you all fuck off?' I said. 'I've got enough on my hands with this woman.'

'Just leave me *alone*,' the woman said, looking like my grandmother on one of her sick days. My grandmother died when I was sixteen. She always suffered from chronic asthma, and one day her muscles just gave up the effort. Perhaps this was her, coming back to haunt me. She always said she wanted to tan the hide off me. Maybe this was her, in her hide-tanning form?

Then, I suppose in desperation, the woman slapped me. It was a real backhander, across the mouth. The slap brought me back to my senses. It stung and I was embarrassed. I was embarrassed for the old man, and I let her lead him back towards the supermarket. 'I hope he lives a long time,' I said. Then I climbed in the car and went back to my house, and I apologised to the squatters for not getting food in, but I didn't think I was welcome at the supermarket.

Maybe I was cracking up at that point, I don't know. I hoped I wasn't, because I really didn't have time for it, God knows, I had enough on my plate. But clearly things were strange in my life, and it was time to start making some sense of them.

The biggest change was through the squatters, who, as I've mentioned, in some ways were the least of my problems. But it has to be said, they had arrived, and they had arrived at an unfortunate time. Maybe for a year I had coped with my loss, because truly there was no real alternative. I had nothing to do but keep living my life and report to my office, and I had the occasional affair. Monica Thorson was witness to that, and she'd say she's the best thing I had. She was wrong, of course, I didn't need Monica, I wasn't even sure that I liked her. But that's how my life was intended to be, just working and sleeping and – 'Monica'. Unless something happened there was no need to change it; and the squatters, of course, were that something.

I'd coped with loss for the length of a year now, which meant I had not truly faced it. Maybe the squatters were a pointer to elsewhere, perhaps someplace else I was welcome. God knows what kind of relationship we had, the main thing I know is that I worried for them. They didn't appear to take care of themselves properly; and they seemed to have slipped into the doldrums. I was trying to take care of them, without knowing what they wanted. I wished they would give me some guidance.

In truth, they demanded precious little from me, except they were fond of my company. I make this assumption because, with very little direct conversation, I have to judge from what they choose to display.

They have been with me for almost three weeks now, and appear to have grown rather morose. After their initial forays into my bedroom and foodstuff, much of their energy seems to have dissipated. They have never been into my bedroom again, nor do they make use of the bathroom. They use the garden for their toilet, a practice I have tried to discourage. But it is as if certain areas are rather taboo to them; as if I must have my own privacy. I should like to explain to them that this is not necessary but, as I've said, we have little conversation.

The business of the foodstuff was rather alarming because, following their initial depredation they have never repeated the exercise, and sometimes they went for two days without eating. This is clearly not healthy, particularly for the woman, but it is difficult to know how to please them. I began to buy in extra foodstuff, and I bought things which I seldom stock for myself. I leave it in piles around the house and it's clear that the squatters appreciate that it's theirs, but sometimes they choose not to eat it. Sometimes they take out the things that they want and, sometimes, they put a few back again. I assume that these offerings are presents for me; but I cannot keep track of their preferences. I think what I intend to do is make a list of every foodstuff, and they can mark off the goods that they need. Maybe this way we'll come to an understanding. Otherwise, I fear for their welfare.

On the matter of rooms, this is fairly defined now, and we each have a space which we stick to. Although even this has begun to alter, as the squatters now actively pursue me. Wherever I linger, their camp-site is rooted, and it's clear that they value my presence. Their main camp-site is beneath the stairwell, but of an evening, while I'm watching the TV, they abandon it to sit round the sofa. They have developed the very annoying habit of changing the channel mid-programme. This got to the point where it became so irritating I had to confiscate the remote control from them. So what I do now is leave open the TV page, and they indicate the programmes which please them. In this way, we all watch together.

But, I have to confess, it can be quite distracting to have them sitting around my ankles. If they are in a particularly energetic mood I am constantly having to step over them. This makes the squatters appear somewhat smaller and I, as if by contrast, seem larger. They accompany me by creeping behind me, and often go down on all fours. At first it was amusing, but that has worn off now. I wish they'd display some more dignity.

Their influence and, indeed, their increasing dependence, has not gone unnoticed by the neighbours. John, who lives opposite, is obviously curious to know more about them, and I often see him peering from his garden. I have not yet, directly, proposed an explanation, but I think people believe they are lodgers. However, I find it increasingly difficult to carry out my own life around them. Not because the squatters make obstacles, but because I feel guilty for leaving them. Today I have come to an important decision: I shall not go out visiting without them. This is a good day to put this plan into operation, for today I am due at a dinner party.

The dinner party was partly the reason I made my trip out to the supermarket. I did not want to take my good wine to the party, I went down to *Gateways* for cheap stuff. Monica is due to attend the dinner party, and she makes it a habit to go cheaply. This is a habit I'm prepared to go along with. I begrudge my good wine on such yuppies.

Monica's presence presents some dilemma, since she still does not know of the squatters. I know what she'll say; it will all be hysterical; and frankly, I'm not really interested. The truth is, as I may have already hinted, I'm just not too sure about Monica. I don't think I like her, I think I've been hoodwinked, I think I liked her because that's what she told me. She has a lot of good qualities, but I suspect probably not enough to sustain me. It might be no coincidence that this realisation coincided with death's anniversary. But maybe I'm ready to face a few truths now. Maybe I needed a year to grow stronger.

I put a call in to my hostess at a little after three in the afternoon.

'Josie?' I said, as she answered the telephone. 'It's me, I have something to ask you.'

'What is it, darling?' she said, hardly listening.

'Is it okay if I bring a few people along?'

'People?' she said, on the alert now. 'What kind of people? How many are there? I've already got all the food in.'

'I know. I'm sorry. There are three of them, but they really won't eat much. In fact, they won't even sit at our table.'

'What are they?' she said. 'Some kind of religious fanatics?'

I said, 'No, they're just very self-centred.'

'Self-centred?' she said.

'Well – self-contained. They won't want to join in with the party.' (I don't think so. I *hoped* they wouldn't join in the party.)

'You make them sound like some kind of freaks.'

'You might like them. I think. I'd be grateful.'

'Okay then,' she said. 'But I hope they don't expect much. I can't spread the food out too thinly.'

'You are a sweetheart.' I hung up and turned to the squatters. 'Did you hear that?' They just looked at me, but that's what they always do. 'I'm going to leave the car open, so if you want to come, you'll have to be in there.'

I don't think the squatters were retarded or anything. It would have been unusual to say the least for three companions to be mentally handicapped, unless they'd run away from somewhere. They didn't have the Down's Syndrome look. No, I think they'd made a pact, come to some kind of decision about the world. They had turned their backs on us. Given us the v sign. We weren't worth bothering about any more. I had the idea that maybe the squatters lived in this beautiful fantasy world, where everything was flowers and light. The sort of place dreamed up by someone in the sixties, someone from the hippie generation. I don't know. It's just that they didn't appear stupid, they didn't look stupid. They merely looked a little spaced out (yet I hadn't seen any evidence of drugs, and where would they get them, there wasn't any money around?) And they seemed uninterested in life. Apathetic, maybe. But even that wasn't the right word. I think the best way I can put it is this: they had handed in their notice to the world, resigned, so to speak, just before they were due to be sacked. They knew they were heading for a fall, that they couldn't keep up with the rest of us rats in the race, so they said screw you Jack, I couldn't give a diddycoy's cuss who gets there first, I'm not even going to bother to finish the course – and they stepped off the running track.

That's what I think, but I could be wrong.

DOG PEOPLE: SEVEN

The dinner party was not a success; but not through any fault of the squatters.

They were impeccable. It was my friends who let me down.

They thought it was a joke. They thought I'd *hired* these people. Monica couldn't make it; she would have known that it wasn't a joke. But those people thought it was brilliant. They thought the whole night was a 'hoot'.

The squatters politely sat at their table in the corner, eating the things which Josie had put out for them. They didn't speak at all, they simply munched through the things they were given, and occasionally they looked at us over their shoulders. They didn't do anything. They didn't even object when Josie's dog came in the room and started snarling around them.

I objected. I stood up and said, 'Get that bloody dog away from there.' But the yuppies and cityites around the dinner table thought it was brilliant. They giggled and guffawed and said what a card I was. I could have killed them all.

Josie and George are the type of people who collect expensive ornaments and rich friends, and have great difficulty in telling them apart. The glazed figurine entitled 'Check Mate' by Sarah Bloch (Number 5 of 25) on the sideboard was as important to them as Samantha and James Willoughby, their 'dearest' friends. Had someone told Josie and George that they had to choose between Sam and Jim, and their statuette by Bloch, they would have gone into a flat spin and the issue would never have been resolved. It would have been, for them, an impossible choice.

They only really tolerated me because of Monica. Monica ranked marginally above the bust of U Thant, but somewhat below the antique grandfather clock – which was fairly high for someone on her income. Without Monica to escort me, I would have come between the kitchen mop and the dog's dish. The dog itself was, of course, a show piece: an Afghan hound with a neurotic and temperamental disposition. I think they would have preferred him to be made of porcelain, rather than hair and flesh, but you can't parade china dogs up and down the neighbourhood, so they put up with the messy side of him.

The dinner party urged the mindless dog on, they were tossing it titbits, realising it had a purpose after all. They could use it to bait these funny people and entertain themselves.

The squatters stoically tried to ignore it all.

'Where did you find them?' one of the women asked me. She was a stuck-up yuppie with a face like a kidney, and I should have said, 'Where did you get your face from?'

But of course I didn't. I was awkward. All I could say was, 'This isn't a joke you know. These people are really living in my house.' Which was considerably more than I'd let any of those grinning bastards do. Then the woman wanted to know where she could get one. 'I want to have a squatter, too,' she said. 'I want to take them to dinner parties.' The whole table thought that was brilliant.

'You think this is funny?' I said. 'These people have nowhere to live. They came into my house because it was cold in the garden, and there's nowhere around there they can stay. I didn't bring them here just so you lot can laugh at them. I brought them here because they are lonely.'

The table erupted. If I was a professional comedian I couldn't have got better laughs; everything I said was a wisecrack. Josie's husband stood up and, not very discreetly, began to gather any valuable ornaments from around the room.

'I'll just put these in the other room, while I remember,' he said to Josie. 'You'll recall we have to get a valuation for the insurance people.'

Josie went red when she saw me staring at George, but nodded. Someone else whispered rather too loudly, 'George always uses words like 'recall' when he's nervous – words you normally only see in print. He doesn't trust these tramps.'

George did not really trust anyone, not even himself. Accountants are often like that. They see the whole world as a threat to their financial security. George has nothing but possessions. We used to meet in a pub at Lincoln's Inn Fields at one time, by accident, during lunch hours. We had the misfortune to work in the same area of London at the time. Our awkward conversations revealed to me that Josie was a good asset because of her family connections (something he could not keep to himself because he believed it was impressive) and that she gave out rarely between the sheets. He was always staring lustfully at other women and playing with himself in his pocket. Josie, he told me one Christmas, in an advanced drunken state, had an ice crevice between her legs. When it thawed, which was only on state occasions and public holidays, it melted away to a chasm. He told me rather gloomily, 'You have to swing the old johnnie around quite a bit if you want it to ever touch the sides.' George maintained he was 'very well read', but had never picked up a novel in his life. "Financial Times', old boy. Nothing of importance in any novel that isn't picked up by the pink pages. Stock Market wouldn't fall a single point if another word of fiction was never written. See what I mean?'

He thought films like '1984' and 'Brazil' were humorous.

'Bloody funny chap, that Orwell. Couldn't stop laughing at the end of nineteen-eighty-whatsit – with the rats? Damn bloody funny, and no mistake.'

Those bits that he didn't find funny, he thought were most probably a good idea.

'Personally speaking. Always considered dictators to be quite a good thing. One mind on the job, no arguments.'

'Like Papa Doc,' I said.

George stared at me with a 'roaming' expression.

'Yes, like him. One set of instructions, no problems, see?'

'And Pol Pot'

'Who?' (He admitted some vagueness.) 'Yes, him too.'

'Hitler?'

George smiled a superior smile. He was on safe ground there. He knew who Hitler was.

'He did give Germany the autobahns and the Volkswagen.'

'So he did,' I said. 'I'd completely forgotten that. And the modern gas oven, too.'

George wagged a finger at me, and smiled.

'Now you are being facetious.'

So, that being George, and Josie being an extension of George's opinions, the 'friends' (including myself?) were not exactly a sensitive group of folk.

I began to get angry after a while, and started picking on the woman with the kidney face. It wasn't difficult to get at someone like her, and even as I was doing it I was feeling guilty.

'You come along here with a face like that,' I said. 'And then you start laughing at these people? Jesus.'

Like I said, these days I'm getting good at arguments; I pick them at the drop of a pencil.

'You ought to be ashamed of yourself. The only good thing about you is your jewellery, and I bet half of that comes from junk shops. You want to start getting yourself in order, before you try sticking it to somebody else.'

Then her boyfriend took exception, but he was ugly too. Ugliness ran all the way through their lifestyle.

'What on earth's the matter with you?' he said. 'What do you have to get so personal for?'

'Personal?' I said. 'I'm not getting personal. I'm just trying to tell you what I feel like. You sit there like Pharaoh and you think you have the right to make judgements on people. Who the hell told you that you could make judgements? You can't even eat with your mouth closed. At least those three people have some kind of manners.'

Most of the laughter had died out by this time, and there was an uncomfortable silence around us. I think the silence was what encouraged me, because I stood up and threw down my napkin.

'I believe I've had enough of this,' I said. 'I didn't come here to have these people insulted, I came here because they were hungry. I didn't bring them here for you to poke fun at. I think that you're all disgusting.'

'Now just sit down a minute – ' somebody said.

'Oh sit down yourself, you moron.' That was a rather pointless one, because the guy had not left his seat yet. But I was getting into some kind of rhythm by that time, and I didn't want to waste it by quibbling.

'What the hell's got into you?' somebody said.

'Nothing's got into me. *You* people have got into me. You're all sitting there like despots. It's not a fucking game, you know, these people are trying to survive.'

'What are you talking about, they're eating smoked salmon.'

'And we're sitting here eating oysters. Don't talk to me about personal sacrifice, I lost my whole family!'

That brought an even longer silence, and people started looking uneasy.

'Is that what it's all about?' someone murmured.

'It's nothing,' I said, sitting down. 'Just forget it.' Suddenly I didn't want to talk any more. I wanted everyone to start eating, so that the only sound would be the click and clack of bronze cutlery on expensive china. I stared down at the willow pattern, hating it. There's always a pair of lovers in a willow pattern. I hoped the bridge would collapse under the weight of the boy-lover and drown him, before he got into worse trouble on the other side of the plate, where the girl-lover was waiting. Bloody willows, bloody doves, or whatever they were.

'Everyone's sorry that you lost your family - '

'Just forget it!' I said. 'Forget it!' I stood up and began to pace around the table, and no one looked towards me. 'Have you asked their names?' I said. 'These people you think are a comedy.' They had never told me their names, so I made them up as I pointed to each one of them. 'This one is John,' I said, my finger on the bearded one. 'And this is Theresa, and Michael. They've all got names, they're not just objects.' (The squatters were looking rather embarrassed and bemused.) 'They all have a name and a history. They give me a lot, you know. They give me companionship. And that's more than I can say for your company. What do you give me? Oysters and gateau! Do you think that makes up for the silence?'

'What silence?' said someone.

'The whole world is silent! You don't even know what the world is!'

'Why don't you take them home?' someone asked me. And I thought they were right, I was crying.

I don't know why I'd started to cry; whether it was frustration, or anger, or sadness. But the sound of my sobbing was a terrible thing, and no one could finish their eating.

Even the squatters, who'd been eating like horses, put down their knives and sat watching.

'You're probably right,' I said, wiping the tears away. 'I'm sorry if I mucked up your evening.' I shouldn't have said that, it made them forgive me. I think I preferred their anger.

'Come on,' I said, aiming my words at the squatters; but they were already standing in the doorway. I started to say something, then realised it was pointless, and walked out of the door without speaking. And I cried again as the night hit my face.

We returned along the A127 and a dull rain came down like cold misery. I pulled up at what I thought was the tree-stump, and said, 'That's the tree where my wife died.'

For a long time there was nothing but silence in the car, just the silence, the rain and the wiper blades. Then one of the squatters leaned out of the window and stabbed at the bark with his penknife. Then he got out of the car and kicked at the stump, and picked up a handful of grass which he lay on it. And then he tried setting fire to it.

It was pouring with rain and big bearded John was trying to light a tree-stump with a box of Swan Vestas. I smiled and said, 'Get back in the car, John.' (I don't even know if that's the stump.)

The following morning I started making phone calls, to the guests who had been at the dinner party. They thought I was phoning to make an apology, but all that I said was, 'You're over.' Some of them queried it and asked what I meant by it. I patiently told them that our friendship was over. Life had been steady, and now it had gone haywire. I ended that life with a vengeance.

I went out into the garden and walked through the long grass. By then there was another frost on the ground and the weeds were so brittle they broke like sacrificial twigs beneath my heels. I was beginning to enjoy breaking things up; Ford Escorts, parties, friendships, affairs, job prospects and other people's lives.

Everything has a winter, when matters become frozen and inflexible, and if you start kicking at that point, they shatter. I wondered about grief: that seems to have no other season *but* winter. I wanted to shatter grief, but I didn't know where to kick, how to go about it. But maybe if I tried hard I'd discover its weak spot. Maybe I'd know what to do then.

DOG PEOPLE: EIGHT

Two days later Monica called round, on a mission of comfort and mercy.

She was looking rough, her hair was ragged, which is not how one normally sees her. Monica's arrogant, she takes pride in her body, she gets made-up before eating breakfast. She won't bring the milk in before her hair's perfect. She won't pick the mail up unmanicured. She is a bit plastic really, but it does seem to suit her. Although it can be disconcerting to wake in the night and find that Barbie is asleep right beside you.

It came as something of a shock to see that Monica was human, that she had normal skin underneath it all. I wondered if she was having a nervous breakdown or something.

'What's the matter?' I said.

'Nothing,' said Monica. 'Nothing's the matter. At least, nothing's wrong with my life.' She was standing in the doorway, and the garden spilled out from her like a green train for her entrance. 'It's you I'm worried about,' she said softly. 'It's you that your friends are concerned about.'

'Me?' I said. 'What's wrong with me?' I wondered what rumours were circulating.

'Look at you,' she said, as her eyes wandered over me. 'You look like you've given up washing.'

I let my eyes follow her own long appraisal and had to confess it was true, I had often looked better. 'I'm getting a bit lazy,' I said. 'I've not had a shave yet. I have to get some clothes from the laundry.'

'You're looking disgraceful,' she said. 'No one would recognise you. You look as though you've gone to pieces.'

'That's nonsense,' I muttered. 'I'm just doing other things at the moment. I'm going to get a bath in a minute.'

She watched me for a long time and I saw tiny tendrils of breath curling out of her nostrils. She had a thin jacket on; she looked to be shivering. A cold winter sun made her hair gleam.

'Are you going to ask me in?' she asked.

'Yes, of course,' I said. 'I'm sorry, I'm miles away. Come into the kitchen for coffee.'

I let her in and closed the door behind her, and I followed her out through the dining room. We stood like two dolls in the kitchen. 'I'll put the kettle on,' I murmured.

'Where are they?' she asked.

'Who?' I said.

'The squatters. I was told all about them.'

'Oh,' I said, over the sound of the tap's running water. 'The squatters. They're out in the garden.'

Monica nodded, and looked gravely beyond the large window. 'In the garden. Have they moved from the house now?'

'No,' I said, as I plugged in the kettle. 'They're doing some repairs to the hedgerow. They must have decided the fence is dilapidated. They've started to fill in the openings.'

Monica sighed and took off her jacket and tossed it onto one of the work-surfaces. She was looking quite normal; she'd dispensed with her arrogance. She ran her long fingers through her hairstyle.

'They're really rather useful,' I said. 'They help keep the place in good order.'

'Oh, Steven,' she sighed. 'What on earth's happening? I heard about the scene at the dinner party.'

'That was nothing to do with me.' I shrugged. 'Did they tell you it was they who were bastards?'

'They're not bastards,' Monica said, sighing and shaking her head in frustration. 'They're your friends, Steven; they're all very worried about you. They're frightened you'll do something stupid.'

'Not me.' I said, watching the steam from the kettle. 'For the first time I feel rather peaceful.'

'God Almighty,' she muttered, but not with an anger. 'How long are they planning to stay here?'

'I've no idea,' I said. 'I've never asked them. I suppose, until they find something better.'

'Can I have a look where they're sleeping?' she asked me.

'I'd rather you didn't. I haven't tidied up yet.'

'You haven't tied yourself up,' she muttered. 'Haven't you noticed what a slob you're becoming?'

'I had observed that,' I said, 'to be honest. I'd noticed some moderate changes. It's just rather little things, like the wrong clothes for the office. And it's hard to get round to getting shaved now. I wouldn't worry about it, it's nothing too major. I seem to find I have more time for other things.'

As I spoke, Monica was moving, and she pushed open the doors to the living-room. 'Oh my God,' she said. 'This place is awful. What kind of life are you living here?'

I followed her to the doorway and we stood looking in on it, and it did look like some kind of bedlam. The squatters had spilled out, their laundry was drying. There was a thick bed of straw on the carpet. 'What, in God's name, are you doing to this place?'

We sat on the edge of the sofa and she gently took hold of my hand. 'Steven, it's awful, it looks like a pig-sty. The smell in here's really appalling.'

I nodded. 'It just needs some tidying.'

'It doesn't need tidying. The whole place looks as though it needs burning.'

'I'm sorry, I said. 'But I do kind of like them. I don't want to have to evict them.'

Something stirred amongst the bedding and a small tousled face looked towards us.

'What is *that*?' said Monica, rising to her feet.

'It's a goat. They must have brought it yesterday.' The goat came towards us, a tiny black animal, and Monica's face took on a look of horror.

'Steven, it's crapping on the carpet!'

'They put the straw down to collect it.' I stood up and stepped towards the goat, which only came up to my knee-caps. 'It's really quite endearing, do you see how it stares at you? Watch this - ' And I knelt down and called it.

The goat came towards me on hesitant footsteps, and I touched it behind its pricked ears. 'It's very gentle,' I said, as the goat started suckling and wrapped its soft lips around my fingers. 'I think it must be very young. I've never had an animal before.'

'But it's a *goat*!' said Monica. 'Look at this - it's chewed up your sofa!'

'It's only a sofa,' I murmured, still stroking. 'The thing's a baby. It's probably nervous.'

'Oh my God.' Monica turned away and sighed, and sat in an armchair by the window. 'What is going on with you Steven? Why are you messing up your life?'

'I'm not,' I said. 'I'm trying to be friendly. I'm trying to help out these people.'

'But what about your own life? What's happening to that?' she said. 'Why haven't you gone to the office?'

'I took a few days off,' I said. 'I've not had a holiday in a long time.'

'But this isn't a holiday!' said Monica. 'This is insanity! You look like you're having a breakdown.'

I said nothing. Some things take too long to account for. I let the goat keep sucking on my fingers, and Monica went to make coffee.

It's true, I had no interest in work now, and I could not go into the office. It's strange, but Malcolm J was off, also, and I've never known him to take any sick leave. He was laid up with something, it had to be serious, bubonic plague would not normally detain him. Malcolm J could make the whole office into invalids, but he'd still make damn sure he was present. It was like a man I'd once encountered who had an affair with a woman. The affair was extended, it went on for ages, but the man would not leave for the mistress.

The mistress became rather jealous of the wife, and she did all she could to entice him. But he wouldn't have it, he wouldn't break his home up, and the mistress must have gone kind of crazy. She started sleeping around a lot, with any sick man she could find. She must have slept with every loser, until she contracted the killer disease AIDS. Then she infected her lover. And he then infected his own wife. When he said to her, 'Why did you do this to me? Why did you want me to destroy my own wife?' – the mistress said simply, 'Because I was jealous.' 'But you've destroyed me, too,' he said. And the woman agreed with that, and she already had an answer. She said, 'But my jealousy's boundless.'

That was what Malcolm J Barnett was like, he'd infect you, but he'd keep on working.

Another development at the office was that I'd made some real progress on Adams. I'd finally got the Inspector to tell me what it was they were pursuing. It seems Felix Adams had conducted a deal with a businessman somewhere in Jersey. The deal was a private one, it didn't go through the records, they set up some weird kind of cover. The money wasn't paid into Adams's own name, it was paid as dividends through a company in Australia. And the dividends weren't registered to Adams himself, they were put in the name of his first son-in-law, who is Syrian, and lives in Aleppo. It took a long time for these details to come out, and now the Inland Revenue Fraud Squad was investigating. It gave me no pleasure to find out these details, the money had still not been traced yet. I was sure that his wife had not come into the money and, for all I know, it's still in Aleppo. I had to unravel it, but I'd lost all my interest. I think that was what made me go absent.

I looked up from my thoughts as Monica came back and put coffee on the table before me. She seemed very calm, and this rather surprised me; I was used to her being more assertive. I wondered if maybe we'd been mistaken, that there was more to our life than I realised. I wondered if it was too late to debate it.

'Why don't you tell me about the squatters?' she said. 'Perhaps I can help you explain it.'

'There's not much to tell,' I said. 'They don't seem to want much. They just seem to like being near me. Last night I was having a soak in the bathtub, and the bathroom's the one room they steer clear of. They are usually waiting for me when I come out of it, they're there in a heap on the carpet. They just seem to like to sit close to where I am. They press themselves up to the keyhole.

'Last night I was lying there, I was thinking about Angela. It's been more than a year since she died now. I've been having hallucinations, I keep thinking I see her. And Matthew, my son, is there too. They've been there a long time, but now they just look at me. I don't know quite what they're expecting.

'When I'd been in there for the best part of an hour, I could hear someone picking at the door-lock. It was just tiny scratching sounds, not really forcing. They were trying to come into the bathroom. I guess it was kind of a doomed enterprise, there was no way they could get at the handle. But it became quite pathetic as I watched them attempt it, they were poking through things like old fuse-wire. And then they straightened out a coathanger, and they tried to unfasten it with that. It was like children, really, playing at burglars; they couldn't get anything through the door-jamb. I could picture their faces; their utter frustration; the shock of their own limitations. Finally I couldn't stand the waiting any longer, and I reached over and slid back the door-catch. Then they came in, and sat down by the bathtub. And they didn't do anything but watch me. Then it seemed like we'd bypassed the last of the hurdles. And, now, I have no secrets from them.'

I didn't say more on it, because there wasn't much *to* say, we merely sat on the sofa, being silent.

The goat grew bored by my inactivity and began prancing up and down in the straw. Then it started eating an old Devil's Ivy, and I was aware that the room's life was threatened. But I didn't really mind that; the goat was endearing. I've never been close to an animal.

Monica sighed and lit a cigarette, and I was conscious of how soft she'd become. There was none of her raging and none of her tantrums. She genuinely seemed quite concerned.

'Is this all connected with Angela?' she asked me. 'Are you having a bad time with your nightmares?'

'No,' I said, 'the nightmares are okay. I don't get them too often now.' I didn't explain that I had them twice weekly, and sometimes woke up from them screaming. Nor did I want to say too much about Angela, because Monica still finds that awkward. I suppose it must be difficult to be mad for somebody when a part of them still lingers elsewhere. She knows that I miss her, and in a way that must hurt her. It's something I try not to talk about.

'You can't go on like this,' she said. 'There has to be an end to it somewhere.'

'I know.' I was waiting for the start of a tirade against squatters, but Monica wasn't delivering it. I've known her a year now, and thought that I knew her; but this was a mystery to me. I was exceptionally glad of her silence.

'I can understand your wanting to help them,' she said. 'But you can't act as if they are animals. This living in straw, and creeping around after you – really, I don't think it's healthy. I don't think it's good for them to become too dependent. They ought to hold on to their dignity.'

'I know,' I said. 'I've thought of that. But the woman is pregnant, there's nowhere to go. I can't have them simply evicted.'

'We could try to get some – some help,' she said. 'We could look for advice from somebody.'

'Maybe,' I said. 'But maybe they don't want it. They seem kind of happy in this house.'

'Why don't we go away for a few days?' said Monica. 'Give ourselves time to think it over.'

'Where would we go?' I said.

'We've often talked about Ely. Why don't we go there? You've got a few days off. Why don't we drive there tomorrow?'

'What about you?' I said.

'I'll take some time off. We both need a break from our habit.'

I thought about it. It seemed a good idea. I'd like a few days to consider.

'What about the squatters?' I said. 'Who's going to look after them?'

'They managed all right before you came.'

She was right. I didn't know the squatters' history, but they'd managed to come this far unaided. 'I'll have to leave the keys with them.'

'Do anything. Let's just enjoy it.'

'Yes,' I said, nodding, watching the goat feed. 'I think I'd like some time to ponder.'

'We'll go in the morning, then. I'll make the arrangements. You explain things to the squatters.'

'Okay,' I said, standing as she put her cup down. 'I'll get a few items together. I've got a lot to do, I think, I haven't got any clean clothes to wear. I'll have to do some rapid laundry. I'll show them how to work all the gadgets.' I was growing excited; the squatters could do it; they could prove they could live quite successfully. 'It's a good idea,' I said. 'I think they deserve it. I think they would like to be normal.'

'I'm doing it for us, not the squatters,' said Monica.

Monica was leaving as the telephone rang, and it was Bernard Franklyn calling from the office.

'Why aren't you in work today?' he said.

'I've taken a few days off.'

'I know you've taken a few days off, I want to know what's made you do it. You never take time off, not without warning. Is everything all right with you, Roberts?'

'Yes sir, it's fine,' I said. 'I just needed time off. I have a few things to go over.'

'But what about the Adams case? Who's handling that one? We can blow our entire reputation on this.'

'I know, sir. I've got it in order.'

'You fill me with confidence.' (His tone was sarcastic.) 'The Revenue's angry. And I'm angry. You've screwed it up, haven't you?'

I sighed and sat down on the floor with the telephone cradled in my lap. 'I haven't done anything. Barnett was handling it. I only took it up when Adams died.'

'I don't care who did it; this one is a bombshell. If you'd had any sense you would have taken the file with you. This is no time to look for a holiday.'

Franklyn hung up then and the squatters came in laughing. I hoped Franklyn never heard about this one.

DOG PEOPLE: NINE

I let Monica make all the arrangements. She's good at that sort of thing. Actually, I think it's Pamela who's the real organiser and Monica who's good at saying what she wants done. Anyway, they are a very efficient team and get things accomplished between them, with Monica saying, 'Book me a weekend in Ely somewhere will you Pam sweetheart? Thanks.' And Pamela telephoning, sending cheques, calling the Ely tourist office for details of sights to see and things to do, checking that the car documents are up to date and that a service has recently been carried out, making sure Monica has packed her toothbrush, all that kind of thing. Monica is one of life's natural leaders, who knows what she wants but communicates nothing, and Pamela is a natural lieutenant who anticipates those unspoken wants to the last detail. Pamela likes being the dogsbody, having someone rely on her efficiency, knowing that if she did drop dead tomorrow, she bloody well *would* be missed. Pamela likes being indispensable. Monica likes having someone do the mundane things in life, without having to fuss about asking for them to be done. ('If you have to explain everything you might as well do it yourself.') Had Pamela been less psychic and unable to read minds, Monica would have said of her, 'She's totally useless that girl. I have to tell her *everything.* No initiative, no common sense.' As it was, Monica called Pamela her 'precious jewel' her 'little treasure' because Pamela *was* paranormally perceptive. I think, to be honest, she was wasted on Monica. She should have been an American President's aide at the very least. In fact, she could even be President.

Before we set off for Ely I left the telephone number of The Black Hostelry on a pad by the phone, so the squatters could call me if they needed something. I also left some money which I borrowed from Monica, in case they ran out of anything. (My own bank manager was being a bastard as usual, treating the bank's money as if it were his own, and refusing to let me extend my overdraft.)

The Black Hostelry (according to the brochures we picked up) was the quarters the old monks used to use when there were monks in Ely Cathedral. It was now a boarding house of the kind that Americans go into raptures over: a medieval monstrosity of oak panelling and architectural warps. ('Well, will ya look at that fireplace. Not a straight line in it. Must be as old as all hell.')

We drove up through Suffolk, into Norfolk and I kept a keen eye open for Ely. According to my old geography master, Mr Simes, Ely rose out of the swamps of the Fens. In those days I had a picture in my head of an Ely like the monster from the black lagoon, a lump of evil rising up through the marsh mists. I was very disappointed after braving hothouse upon hothouse of Norfolk lavender nurseries, with Monica stopping every five minutes to exclaim over some different variety, to find that Ely did not rear dramatically, dripping monster slime, but merely loomed in a townish sort of way.

'That's the 'lantern',' said Monica, pointing out a stumpy tower, an octagonal structure on the top of the cathedral roof. 'It's made of eight oak trees covered with lead.'

I stared up through the windscreen.

'Must weigh tons,' I said. 'I hope that thing isn't above our bedroom, or I'm sleeping in the car.'

'You're such a pleb sometimes.' Monica wrenched the wheel round to take a corner. 'Can't you for once appreciate artistic beauty without making some inane comment? That tower is one of the finest engineering feats of the Middle Ages.'

'Does that make it any lighter?' I queried, raising an eyebrow. 'Besides which, it's ugly. Just because the bloody thing's old and took ten thousand men to lift it up there, doesn't make it a marvellous work of art.'

'Have it your own way,' she said.

We turned into the cathedral car park and Monica stopped the car. Then we gathered the luggage and trooped around to The Black Hostelry, which lay adjacent to the cathedral. The hostelry was a greystone affair with arches all over it, doorways included. We knocked. A woman answered.

'Yes?'

She looked like Jane Austen's Fanny Price would have looked like in her forties, if she had had to rent out rooms in order to finance repairs to her husband's church. Prim, slightly soured, hiding a natural kindness under a layer of bitterness. I have always despised Fanny Price and I think Miss Austen did too. The goodness of Fanny Price is brittle toffee. Not the sort of goodness that melts in the mouth; the kind which snaps and crunches into tiny sweet fragments. Fanny Price is one of those women whose reactions would convince a park flasher that it's been worth all the hassle. Fanny Price is not too good to be true, she is too good to be fiction. Give me Emma anytime. I like a woman who makes mistakes and refuses to admit them.

I came back to myself. 'Rooms,' I said, in an attempt to keep our conversation monosyllabic.

'Name?' she returned, as if she knew the game.

'Mr and Mrs a-hem Smith.'

Monica looked furious. 'The booking was made under Monica Thorson,' she said.

'Yes,' I confirmed. 'Made under and about to be executed by.'

Monica looked at me as if she knew exactly who it was that she wished to see executed.

The woman took little notice of all this. She led us in, showed us the 'suite' and told us that we should indicate whether we were in or out by the little wooden monk on the stairway, who had a sliding IN/OUT tummy.

'The toilets are downstairs,' she said. 'There are no facilities up here. You have a bathroom of course, but no loo in the rooms.'

We were left alone, to a mixture of modern junk (an old fashioned coiled-wire electric fire, a cracked jug, a tatty bookcase, a Woolworth's table lamp) and ancient building (sloping floor, indented arches, low doorways, crumbling brickwork). There were two rooms and a bathroom. The living-room looked down 'on the bishop's garden' (so the brochure said) and we could see a rhubarb jungle and neat rows of over-wintering bean sticks. Did the bishop really do all that, or was some minor member of the clergy responsible for shovelling horse manure onto the rhubarb? I have never liked claims from people who throw out orders, like Monica, while others do the job. 'Mr Wellygogs built the Western Pacific Railway.' No mention of the Chinese immigrants who hefted the steel rails and dug in the sleepers.

The living-room wasn't bad, I had to admit.

The bedroom was dark and gloomy and the only window looked up onto that damn lead lantern thing. The bed looked as though it had been constructed at the same time as the monastery, and you couldn't squeeze a cat into the bathroom lengthways, let alone swing it. I fell into a chair, the seat of which sagged to floor level.

'Great place,' I said. Then I noticed a telephone. 'I wonder how the squatters are doing?'

Monica stepped between me and the instrument.

Once we were outside I began to like it. There were cropped lawns in the cathedral close and there was a peaceful air to the scene. I love dreaming spires, the way those bricks and slates shoot up into the sky. I've always had ambiguous feelings regarding stately homes and cathedrals. On the one hand I hate the idea that serfs have sweated and died in order to build something to satisfy some powerful bishop or baron's desire for grandness and opulence, or whatever. Especially stately homes. Bloody great things that would hospitalise an army, yet built for the master and his wife to stroll around in. That's always repelled me, whereas some people appear to embrace the idea of others imperiously lording it over them. (Or maybe they identify with the lord? Perhaps they can only visualise themselves in the role of the king, and forget the beggar?)

Yet I get excited over soaring brickwork, flying buttresses, Norman arches, fluted columns. It annoys me. I wish I could hate it, but I get the same feelings of awe as everyone else. I don't think it's a religious feeling, either. I think it has something to do with still being a caveman inside.

'Where are we going?' I asked Monica, who was striding out.

'Thought we'd look inside.'

I shrugged and followed her round the path.

Monica loves guides and she collared a wandering priest immediately, breaking his holy reverie with, 'How high is the tower? Someone said you can see all the way to Russia from up there? Can you take us up?'

His spiritual communing shattered, the priest began to tell us all about the place.

'The mosaic maze you are standing on – ' we looked down '- is exactly the same length as the height of the tower!' We looked up.

Amazing, I thought, and *so what?*

So, we did it all, we went up the tower, failed to see the Ural Mountains, got frozen in the wind and were tempted to jump. Although possibly that was just me.

We climbed into that monstrous bed about nine o'clock and Monica immediately found the hollows in my body.

'Is this a good idea,' I whispered, 'I mean hallowed ground and all that? There might be some old monks in here with us.'

She began to rub up against me.

'God, you know how to get me excited,' she said, but I wasn't sure whether she meant I was talking dirty, or whether she was being sarcastic. Anyway, we did it, and when our breath began to come out hot and stale, the way it does sometimes, I began to enjoy the physical side of it, even though I knew I would lose the race as usual. I've always had trouble with the mental part of sex with Monica, because I still feel as if I'm committing adultery. Sometimes that can be a positive thing. When I'm feeling guilty I get desperate and throw caution to the winds, and the feeling of total abandonment is good for someone like me, who's normally as taut as a ship's stay. I begin to trawl my partner like a fishing net, touching every part of her body with all the parts of me.

However, there are times when the thought that I'm being unfaithful to my wife extends down to my loins, and then I can have great difficulty. I still manage an erection and (of course) Monica gets there, sometimes smashing her own record. (One of these days I'm going to say, 'Let's make...' and she's going to climax before I even get the final word out.) But there are occasions when I can't even reach orgasm. Monica feels sorry for me at those times, which makes it worse, and tells me I 'can do anything, anything at all' to her, which is supposed to excite me. She suggests positions, but the only one that really works is from behind, with her bottom in the air, because that way her face is buried in a pillow where I can't see it, and she need not be Monica any more.

'There, wasn't that good?' she said afterwards, snuggling up against me.

'Yes,' I replied.

'Well don't go overboard, sailor. I mean there are some men who would kill for what you get on a plate.'

'Maybe that's the trouble. Maybe you should hold out sometimes and make me beg?'

She snorted. 'That's degrading. I don't like that. Anyway, I do say no, quite often.'

'Only in a crowded street,' I said, and she giggled as I suspected she would. Monica is good at forming mental images and I knew she had instantly visualised us having it away in the middle of Southend High Street on a Saturday morning.

'Wouldn't *that* cause a fuss?' she said.

Just before we dropped off to sleep, she murmured, 'I think you're getting better. I'm glad we came here.' And left me wondering whether she intended the *double entendre.*

At three o'clock I woke from a nightmare. The air in the room was still and the darkness *very* still. I could see the moonlight on the cathedral. I needed the shipping forecast man, but we didn't have a radio with us. I promised myself that I would get a cassette and tape a broadcast, so that I wouldn't be without him. (Somehow that wouldn't be the same, though. I need him live and immediate.) Around me the house was gently creaking the way old houses do in the middle of the night, stirring restlessly while we slept, like a patient dog awaiting the waking of its master. I badly wanted to go to the toilet, but there was no way I was going down those stairs to the toilet below. Not alone.

I crept into the bathroom and urinated in the bath, trying to keep the sounds down. When I turned on the tap I heard Monica sigh, but I don't think she woke up.

I got back into bed carefully and lay in the darkness, wondering what the hell I was doing in Ely.

And then a bell went off, and began to ring rhythmically.

'Wha...what's that?' said Monica's voice, from somewhere below the covers.

'The telephone, I think.'

'Well *answer* the bloody thing.'

I reached out and felt around, finding the receiver.

'Hello?' I said.

There was a silence at first, then a male voice said:

'It's coming!'

Then the line went dead.

I jumped out of bed and switched on the light. I reached for my socks and started to pull them on.

'What the *hell* are you doing?'

Monica was sitting up in bed, her breasts over the coverlet.

'I have to go home,' I said. 'The baby's on its way.'

'What bloody baby?'

'One of the squatters – the female.'

'Well I didn't think it would be one of the men.' She stared at me while I struggled with my jeans. 'Though it could be the flaming goat I suppose. Oh, what's happening to you? I can't stand this. You *can't* go home now. Wait until tomorrow. What can you do anyway?' Monica's voice rose. 'What do you know about delivering babies, for Christ's sake? You're not a flaming midwife.'

'They need me,' I said. 'I'm responsible.'

She took that the wrong way.

'You – it's *your* baby?'

'No. Jesus, Monica. I mean it's my house. I'm responsible for what goes on there.'

'You're not responsible for them. They broke into your home. You would have thrown them out if you'd had any sense. It's not your problem, the woman having the thing.'

I paused and looked at her.

'It's not a *thing* – it's a child.'

'Just a figure of speech. How are you going to get there?'

I stopped pulling on my T shirt.

'The car?'

Monica smiled one of her nasty smiles now.

'Not in my car, buster.'

'Well lend me some money then, for a train.'

'You won't get a train at this time of night. Anyway, I gave you some money yesterday.'

I continued dressing.

'I spent it.'

'You haven't had a chance.'

'I left it at home then.'

'For the squatters.'

'Yes,' I said. 'I left it for the squatters.'

'Damn you Roberts.'

'Yes.'

I left the room and stumbled down the stairs and out of the front door into the night. The sacred edifice towered above me as I walked along the gravel path, through the graves, and out onto the pavement. I took my bearings and began walking through the empty streets. When I reached the edge of Ely I studied the signposts and set off again. After a while my legs began to get tired. I wondered if I was going to make it all the way to Essex. There were one or two cars on the road and I tried flagging one down, but it swerved around me. Finally, I got one to stop.

It was Monica.

'Get in,' she said. 'If you keep walking in that direction you'll end up in The Wash.'

'The wrong way?'

'Just a bit.'

'How did you know where to find me?'

'I tried the other way, and I know you. You don't do things by halves. If you get something wrong, you get it completely wrong. Are you going to get in?'

I climbed in the car and she turned it around. We set off for Essex along the dark roads. I tuned the car's radio to BBC4. I had needed to hear the shipping forecast since the nightmare in the monk's cell. I waited for those soft reassuring tones, telling me that even though storms were about to break, all was really well with the world. But the words never came. I suppose it was a bit late, or too early, for the bulletins. Or maybe it was like glass out there on the ocean and the ships' captains had no need of a firm calming voice? Monica said nothing and I switched off the radio.

After we had been driving for two hours, she spoke.

'Damn you, Roberts,' she said.

'Yes,' I replied. 'I know.'

The dawn began to float up like grey silk.

DOG PEOPLE: TEN

It was a false alarm.

When we reached the house, everything was in darkness. I jumped out of the car and unlocked the door to the house. When I got inside I realised the place was too quiet for a birth to be happening, or even to have just been completed. I crept into the living-room to find the squatters standing at the window. I could see their shapes in the near dark, hunched and awkward-looking. They had been waiting for me to come home. I sensed a completeness in the air, as they shuffled away from the window to their area under the stairs. Five o'clock and all is well – all is okay with the world.

Something licked my hand and cried like a baby. But it was only the goat looking for some kind of attention. It tried to eat my trouser-leg and I pushed it gently away from me.

'No baby, eh?' I said to the shapes in the corner.

They hunched closer together, but I could see teeth. One of them must have been smiling at me. For a few moments I thought that it might be a joke: that they were maybe having fun with me. Maybe I would, or should, have been angry that it was such a costly joke. Then I realised I was wrong. I think the smile was a nervous smile, from someone feeling both guilty and relieved. I knew then why they had pretended the baby was on its way. They wanted me *here,* with them. They were miserable when I was away. They were like pets, pining for their master. I understood this.

'Don't worry,' I said, 'I'm not going away again.'

There was an answering shuffle.

From outside came the sound of a car roaring away, spraying gravel. Monica was angry. I went out and found my things strewn all over the driveway. The case had burst open and items of underwear were spread on the ground. I picked them up. The goat had followed me out and managed to get hold of a vest. It was eating it slowly. I pulled it carefully from the animal's mouth because I was afraid it would choke.

'I'll get you some corn flakes,' I told it.

I went back indoors and had the best blessed sleep I had had in a long time. It must have been the tiring journey.

Sunday was quiet, I slept most of the day, but on Monday all hell was let loose.

With the mail came two bombshells. One was from the building society. Someone had squealed on me and they knew there were other people living in the house. They reminded me that according to the mortgage agreement I could not let, sublet or rent out rooms without the permission of the building society. They would be grateful if I would call at their offices in Southend High Street to discuss the matter. Furthermore, they had recently perused the Deeds to the house, which they held and were entitled to view, and was I aware there was a covenant stating that no domestic livestock was permitted on the premises, which included the garden area?

The snitch had been thorough. It was probably the old woman in the big run-down house at the end of the lane. She had never liked me since I fed her ginger cat. In fact she had screamed at me for 'enticing' away the half-starved animal which she wouldn't even allow in the house anyway. 'It's a barn cat,' she had cried, 'it catches mice!' 'But you haven't got a bloody barn!' I had yelled back at her. 'You let the thing starve, and the two dogs. Why do you have animals if you're not going to look after them? The dogs come in here when there's thunder in the air because you won't let them into *your* house. They're your bloody animals, woman!'

The upshot was that a few days later I had a letter from her solicitor and I went out and picked up Hecate, the cat, which had lost an eye through ringworm, had fur coming out, and ribs showing through like a row of little hoops. I put it in the car and drove it into the nearby town of Hockley, carried it into the solicitor's office, and dumped it without ceremony on his desk. 'Take a look at that,' I told him, 'and then see if you can make an enticement claim stick.'

I never heard from him again.

This was that woman trying to get back at me. I bet she had been waiting for something like this for months. I bet she would have waited a million years.

I rang up the building society.

'Mr Braithwaite? Roberts here. I got your letter this morning about my friends. I have some friends staying with me and it's no fucking business of yours whether they are here or not. Okay, I'm sorry about the swearing, but your letter made me angry. No, I'm not charging them any rent. They're friends. They've come for a holiday. What? Yes, they have a goat. I know. They brought it with them. It's not in permanent residence. What? Look Braithwaite, the Deeds specifically state 'no domestic animals'. Well this is a bloody *wild* goat, okay?' I slammed down the telephone, feeling very pleased with myself.

The second bombshell was my credit card account, which looked as if someone had gone crazy with zeros.

I rang them up, too.

'I think it is absolutely immoral to allow someone to build up a debt of this size,' I told a startled manager on the other end, 'knowing full well they can't pay it. You should be ashamed of yourselves. Why didn't you recall the card before I got into such deep water? You're causing me enormous stress.'

'Mr...?'

'Roberts.'

'Mr Roberts, we make every effort to meet our cardholders halfway. If you feel you can't make the minimum repayment then we may be able to find a sum which is within your means. In the meantime, of course, we must ask for the return of the card.'

'Must you?'

'I'm afraid so.'

'What are you afraid of?'

'Mr Roberts, I'm sorry but I can't play word games with you at ten o'clock in the morning.'

'Well, I'll tell you what *I'm* afraid of. I'm afraid of having a nervous breakdown. I bet you're a decent man. I imagine you have a wife and family and treat them nicely. I expect you have a cat or a dog. I'm in trouble. I have four mouths to feed at the moment. Five, if you count the goat. We have a goat for its milk because my friend's pregnant wife is allergic to cow's milk. The baby's due soon. But it's all temporary, see? Nothing is permanent. At the moment the whole house is upside down. I can't think straight. It's bills like yours that make the car exhaust pipe look inviting. You get a piece of hose, see, and all you have to do is connect it to the pipe and put the other end in the window. Then you sit in the car, switch on the engine, and wait. Pretty soon unpaid debts don't matter to you any more.'

There was an uncomfortable silence at the other end, where I was sure the manager was wrestling with himself, trying to decide whether this was a genuine call or whether I was trying it on. Then a voice said softly, 'Mr Roberts, have you considered calling the Samaritans? I've used them myself.'

'You think that's a good idea?'

'I think it's an excellent idea. In the meantime I'll have a word with Head Office about the debt.'

'Do you think...do you think they might raise my limit, just a couple of hundred pounds?'

There was another long silence, then, 'I can't promise that Mr Roberts. All I can say is I'll see what I can do.'

'Thanks, you're a brick.'

'And Mr Roberts – call the Samaritans. They are very good. A year ago I was at my wit's end, and they helped a lot. I had to go into Runwell Hospital for a while too, but without their initial help I would probably – well, just give them a try.'

'I will, thanks again. And you won't forget to ask about the limit...' but the line had gone dead.

I put my thumb up to one of the squatters, who was staring at me from the corner of the room.

'We can hack 'em down like ripe wheat!' I said.

He stared at me wide-eyed.

And at that moment a flaming policeman came crunching over my gravel driveway, to ring the bell.

'What now?' I muttered, wondering whether to ignore it, but he glanced up at the window and saw one of the squatters looking down at him and rang the bell again. I went to the door and opened it.

I was faced by a young man in his early twenties, smoothfaced. He was one of those coppers that make you wonder how the public in the inner cities get the idea that coppers are bent. When you look at policemen like this one, a cherubic choirboy in fancy dress, you can't believe there's corruption in the force, that some of his colleagues might beat people up. He looked more shockable than some of the church-going spinsters in the village.

'Yes?' I said.

'Mr Roberts?'

My heart sank. So it was specifically to do with *me.*

'Yep.'

He looked me up and down and I realised I was in a mess. I still had on my pyjamas, and I was unshaven and barefooted.

'Mr Roberts, we have had a complaint from a Mrs Wittfield...'

'Don't know her,' I said quickly, wondering what was the surname of the woman at the end of the lane.

His face took on a patient thousand-year look, such as the slaves building the pyramids of Egypt must have worn. He realised he had a long and difficult task ahead of him which might not be completed during his lifetime.

'Can we step inside?' he asked.

I moved to fill the doorway.

'I'd rather we didn't – the place is in a state,' I said.

He settled back on his heels.

'The fact is, Mr Roberts, we have had a complaint from a Mrs Wittfield, of Lander's Drive. She said you attempted to kidnap her husband the other morning. Now I've spoken to one or two witnesses and it seems you did rough handle Mr Wittfield.'

'I was trying to help him,' I said. 'The poor old bast--- Mr Wittfield isn't well. I helped him once before, on the sea wall, where he had some kind of attack. When I saw him again outside the supermarket...'

There was a yell from inside the house and the next moment the goat tried to squeeze between my legs. I pushed it back with the heel of my foot, then one of the squatters came and grabbed its horns, leading it back into the living-room.

The policeman's eyes seemed to age another thousand years.

'Our goat,' I said. 'Wild. We're trying to tame it, so we can sell it. Anyway, as I was saying, I was trying to help the old man. He looked kind of lost and I suggested we go down to the pub. He said that he wanted to.'

'Mrs Wittfield informed us that Mr Wittfield has lost the power of speech.'

I grinned.

'Officer, you're a young man. Can you imagine what it's like being married to a woman like that for forty years? You saw her. If she was my wife I'd lose the power to do anything and everything, if you get my meaning.'

His eyes hardened.

'Are you saying he spoke to you?'

'Said he wanted to go for a pint. 'Looking forward to it,' he said. I know Mr Wittfield well. We used to meet on the train, going to work every morning. I can get that verified. Of course, *she* didn't know me, I'd never seen her before. But Mr Wittfield and I were travelling companions. You can get quite close to a man, seeing him every morning for years.'

This got to him. I could see a change in his expression.

'There are people who saw you together?'

'Constable, you only have to ask his wife. It's the eight-thirty from Southend Victoria to Liverpool Street. We both caught it every morning. He used to wear a dark pinstripe and carried a battered old briefcase and an umbrella – a golfing umbrella, one of those with different coloured panels,' I cried triumphantly, as I remembered this detail about him. 'Otherwise, you would have to ask the others who caught the same train. Obviously we don't know each other's names, not all of us. Old Bert, the ticket collector knows us all. He'd tell you.'

The officer's eyes brightened.

'You know Bert?'

I raised my arms.

'Is there anyone who doesn't? When Bert went to the Vatican and had his photograph taken with the Pope, the entire English-speaking world said, 'Well that's Bert on the left, but who's the guy in the robes and the mitre?'

The policeman closed his notebook.

'Look,' he said, 'I'm going to do a little checking round, but in the meantime, no more incidents. We can't have people disturbing the peace in Ashingdon. It's a quiet village, so let's keep it that way.'

'Good morning, constable.'

'Good morning.' He turned to leave, then swung back. 'Why aren't you at work today? It's gone eight-thirty.'

'I'm not well,' I said, rubbing my grizzled chin. 'I'm off sick at the moment. You can ring them if you like.'

He shook his head and continued down the path.

'Bloody hell,' I muttered. 'Can't even give a bloke some help without they throw you in the nick.'

I slammed the door.

So that was Monday. Almost all of it. Monica didn't ring, or she might have done, while I was out. I thought I'd better give the squatters some fresh air, since they seemed disinclined to go out while I remained indoors. I felt I could do with a walk myself, even if it was just up to the top meadow and back. So I put on my coat and waited on the driveway. They all came tumbling out a few moments later, one of them leading the goat on a piece of string.

We took the path up by the old bat's place and I threw a v sign at the window, hoping she was behind it.

At the top meadow it was windy, but we could see the river from there, quite well. There were yachts sailing up and down and one or two barges were gliding through the water. In the field the thistles remained on isolated patches where the cows and horses had eaten around them. In my next life I want to be a thistle. Nobody bothers thistles.

That evening there was a storm in the Bay of Biscay. I listened to the shipping bulletin, gaining some comfort from the fact that the house would not have to go to sea. The squatters crowded around the radio, drinking in the confident tones. I imagined the waves battering the trawlers as they struggled through squalls and high winds, climbing vertical seas, and falling into deep troughs. What a life, but at least they knew they were living.

'Those people are out there,' I said to the squatters, 'going through a mad hell of raging water just to put a few bits of cod into our fish-and-chip shop down the road. Icelandic seas,' I continued. 'Do you know what Icelandic seas are like? Hard to imagine, isn't it, a wave the height of this hill we're perched on now? And that man,' I pointed to the radio, 'keeps everyone calm, helps fight off the panic. I bet there are thousands of landlubbers out there, in London, in Liverpool, who tune into the shipping forecast every night just to save themselves. We don't need the Samaritans, do we? We've got the shipping bulletin man to get rid of our anxiety. I wonder if the mental homes use him? It seems a reasonable idea. They probably gather their patients into one room to listen to him, when there is general unrest in the wards.'

It was a nice picture.

One of the squatters, the woman, woke me at dawn. We were all curled up under the stairs. She had been to the window and she pointed.

I got up and walked over to the French doors, looking out into the grey mists. Then I saw it. The fucking heron. It was eating something on my lawn. I thought about getting my shotgun, then changed my mind. Someone would hear the shot and call the cops. I was in enough trouble as it was. Instead I ran out waving my arms.

'Shoooo. Shooo you bastard, shooo.'

It had some difficulty in taking off, and I thought I might get to it and strangle it, silently. They must be easy birds to choke to death, with necks like that. You could tie a knot in it and just leave it to kick out its last. But it rose in the air just before I reached it. There were bits of koi carp on the lawn, where it had been standing. Probably from the garden centre half-a-mile down the road. They sold koi at three hundred quid a time.

'At least he's graduated from goldfish and tench,' I muttered to the squatters when I got back indoors. 'You can't mess with money though. They'll get him if he keeps that up. The rich don't care whether it's a protected species or not. A quick phone call to the mafia, a contract, and bingo – it's the old wire snare trick.'

I nodded, then an idea came to me, as I thought of my credit card debt.

'I wonder how much they would pay me to wipe out a heron?'

DOG PEOPLE: ELEVEN

I met Malcolm J by accident in Foyles.

I had gone up to London to get a present for Monica. I felt bad about our ruined weekend and I hadn't even had a fluttering phone call since we returned early on Sunday morning. Monday was a pig's orphan, Tuesday not much better, so Wednesday I decided it was time to get out of the house. I caught the eight-thirty to Liverpool Street, so that I could prime Bert in case he was questioned by the policeman. I needed to be remembered as a friend to the man with frost on his head and loss in his eyes.

I said to Bert, casually, 'Bert, have you seen my mate around lately? Mr Wittfield?' and I began to describe him. I wished I knew Wittfield's first name, but I doubt Bert would question that area of ignorance. Wittfield was probably one of those men whose friends and contemporaries habitually called him by his surname. ('Where's Wittfield these days?' or 'Hey, Wittfield. You coming to the firm's do?') I bet even his beetlish wife had forgotten his first name. ('No, Wittfield, not this month, I have a headache.' Or 'Wittfield – Wittfield - oh-oh-oh-oh WITTFIEEEEEELD!')

Bert, on the other hand, had the opposite problem. He stopped my description halfway through with a wave of his grimy hand.

'All you buggers look alike to me, and I'm fed up with bein' called 'Bert.' Me name is Dennis. Why does everyone call me Bert all the time?'

'I don't know, Bert. Anyway, if you see Mr Wittfield, tell him I was asking after him, would you?'

The elderly ticket collector fixed me with his rheumy eyes.

'Tell 'im yerself,' he said, showing his tobacco stained teeth as he retracted his lips.

'That's not very charitable, Bert,' I said, turning as the train came in. He was a funny bloke. He had been there since the beginning of the world, taking tickets and abusing commuters. Every so often he would try to get people to use his right name, but it was a futile exercise. He'd been Bert to everyone since he started work at about thirteen. I suppose he was too shy in those days to protest. Some station master had decided what he would be called and it stuck. It would go on his gravestone when he died, because the vicar was just as keen on village characters as everyone else. I doubt they would put a surname. (So far as I knew, he hadn't got one, or it had been forgotten by him and everyone else). Poor old Bert, who was clearly not Bert, was subjected to an identity crisis every day of his life. I bet even God knew him as Bert. It's a strange kind of world where people like Bert go through their lives without picking up a surname, while people like Wittfield never manage to acquire a first name.

I like travelling up to the city on the eight-thirty when I'm not working. I enjoy looking at the suited ones who are, and being glad I'm not one of them for once. When I retire I'm going to get up every morning, go down to the station, and wave goodbye to the eight-thirty train after watching them all scramble for seats to fall asleep in.

On the way along the track, we passed Hadleigh Castle, just a broken molar of a ruin on one of the high bits of ground. I had a fondness for that ruin. MM used to take me there to rip off my underpants after a disco. She used to do it to me amongst the ancient stones, up against walls that had kept out dark age winters and woolly warriors. On mud floors where hogs and hounds used to fight for the scraps that fell from rustic banquet tables. In recesses where kings had bonked chamber maids when queenie wasn't home. MM and I had added to the history of that castle with its stonework stained by the blood of peasants and knights. We had not added to its dignity, but then it had never had much in the way of that. It was, after all, a place for screaming, grunting, flailing and struggling, whether one was talking about fighting or fucking.

I met Malcolm J as I was searching Foyles' shelves for a book called BORN TO SHOP by Madeline Rosindale. Monica had once said she would like a copy. Shopping was her hobby and Madeline Rosindale's guide made it easier for women like her to find those stores which sold things at twice the price of ordinary high street shops, but whose décor and staff gave them the 'rich bitch' feeling that some women craved like heroin.

A sweaty hand clamped itself on my shoulder.

'Roberts?'

I turned to face him and then wished I hadn't. He looked terrible. I knew I looked bad, but Malcolm J could have stepped out of the wrong end of a horror movie. His eyes had black pouches underneath and were raw-veined. There was a hard crust of saliva in the corner of his mouth, as if he had just woken from sleep and had not had time to wash. He also looked very anxious, or frightened, or something of that nature. Had I not known him I might have called for assistance.

'Got time for a coffee?' he said.

I nodded.

'Just let me buy this book.'

That is easier said than done in Foyles, whose methods of displaying books and paying for purchases belongs to some distant Dickensian era. I never enter Foyles without wondering in which room they have Bob Cratchit locked away, working away with other accountant's clerks on high stools.

We found a café in Soho and ordered coffee. Malcolm J was trembling a little as he lifted the cup to his lips. Then his other hand shot out and damply clamped itself over mine.

'I've got a confession to make,' he said hoarsely.

Oh – God – Malcolm J – was – a – homosexual!

Malcolm J was gay. And he had my hand in a grip that a professional wrestler would have envied. I wanted to scream and run from the place, out into the street. This flabby monster wanted to rape the hell out of me and leave me ragged. I wondered about the book he had bought, still in its wrapping. 'The Home Psychologist'?

'What is it?' I said, squirming.

He took his hand back.

'No, perhaps I shouldn't bother you with my problems.'

'Attaboy,' I said, relieved. 'You save up your confessions for the priest.'

He turned damp eyes on me.

'I thought you might understand. I've always admired you, Roberts. The fact is – I – I seem to be losing control.'

There, it was out. Not gay, but going down.

He continued. 'You're always so cool, so much in command of yourself. Christ,' he wrung his hands together, 'I admire your confidence. Whenever Franklyn calls for me I crap myself. He turns me to jelly. How do you deal with that?'

All at once I felt pity for the poor slob. Malcolm J was a sea-slug in his last life. Sea-slugs have very limited intelligence and very little soul. They almost always go *up* the chain of being in their next life, jumping a few links, because there's not much in the way of evil that a sea-slug can reasonably get up to. It simply lies in the ooze, buffeted by currents, occasionally sucking in disgusting looking slime at one end and depositing similar material out of the other end (both ends look fairly alike). My dictionary describes a sea-slug as a 'creature with a reduced exoskeleton and tube feet for creeping' which is Malcolm J to an echinoderm. It takes a few reincarnations to get rid of the sea-slug mentality and Malcolm J was still on his first. He was human in form, but basic spongy-sausage-slimer inside.

'What you have to do Malc, is put the beast to sleep.'

'Eh?' His tearful eyes were puzzled. There were damp patches on the table where his hands had been.

'Wrestle with your spirit and keep it subdued,' I said. 'Inside you have all this terror, right? This unnamed horror of anything that's not under your direct control. There's no way you can control Franklyn, so you have to control yourself. Suppress that beast inside you, put it to sleep.'

He blinked at me and sprayed the table with moisture.

I sighed. 'Never mind, Malcolm. What's the book?'

'Nothing,' he said, clutching it tightly against his chest.

'SEX FOR BEGINNERS?' I queried.

'No.' But he didn't sound too sure of himself, so I must have got close.

'Anyway, the next time Franklyn roars at you, tell him you think he looks beautiful when he's angry. He likes a bit of cheek sometimes. Likes a man to have spirit. Don't cower. Sock it to him occasionally.'

'I don't think I can do that.'

'In that case, slime his desk once in a while.'

'What?'

'Nothing. Look, I've got to go, Malc. Give my love to Adams and the office. You look *awful,* by the way.'

'So do you.'

'Thanks.'

I left my holothurian workmate to slick the plastic seat of the café stool. Then I caught the next train home.

When I got back the goat was out and eating something in a neighbour's garden. I took it by the collar and led it back to the house.

Sometime during that evening I remembered the book I had bought Monica. I had left it on the table of the café and I cursed Malcolm J, because if he hadn't asked me to be an agony aunt for him I would never have gone for a coffee in the first place.

I went outside to smoke a cigarette and look at the frost on the lawn. It was a crisp night and the pigeons in the trees of my little spinney were restless. I could hear them moving about in the branches above my head. Somewhere in the wildernesses of Essex a fox called to its kind: a chilling rasping screech that was probably an endearment. *Come to mamma!*

There was comfort, somehow, about being out in the darkness with all these things going on. It made me feel as if there was no possibility of death. How could all this suddenly disappear from me, to be replaced by, what, nothing? There was as much chance of me shooting off into space.

In that moment there was a cry from the house.

I turned and looked at the cottage, sensing urgent movements behind the walls. A light went out and then went on again. A hurrying and a scurrying was in progress. People were afraid. Hands were busy doing things.

A terrible scream rang out.

I turned and began running towards its source.

DOG PEOPLE: TWELVE

I have never seen a baby born. When my wife gave birth she didn't want me with her for some reason. Most wives like their husband to be there, to witness the 'miracle' and to have a hand to hold, but she said, 'It's messy, it's ugly, and it's undignified. I don't want you in there, listening to me yell and staring at the mess around my crotch with everyone else in the room. You wait outside and smoke cigarettes, or whatever you're supposed to do. I'm in favour of tradition. I don't want to have to worry about you as well as giving birth. I'd rather you were out of the way.' I put up a feeble protest, but in my heart I really *didn't* want to be in amongst all that pain and stuff. It would have upset me. It would have upset her. And for what? So I could tell Malcolm J that I'd seen a sight that most sensible men would go out of their way to avoid?

However, I do know there is a lot of pushing, a lot of screaming, and at some point you cut the umbilical. (I assume this takes place after it emerges, in case the child elects to stay in there. God knows, if we knew what a life lay ahead of us we'd all want to stay with our mother.) And, generally, someone says, 'Get the boiling water ready!' And there are towels, but I don't know what they're for. I have heard about forceps, inducement and breech birth, but there's usually someone who knows about these things. It usually takes place in a hospital.

This was not happening, though, this time it took place on a corner of my living-room carpet. It isn't supposed to happen this way, there's supposed to be a suitcase packed, we load up the car and head for the hospital. And all the way there you say things like, 'Keep breathing steadily. Count them. Get the watch out and count them.' And then there's a lot of cheek-puffing and blowing by the patient and their sympathiser.

It doesn't happen this way, which is why I started screaming at them. *'She can't have her baby in the living-room!'*

'Why not?' said someone, and then the thought came to me: 'Yes, why not? I suppose there's no reason.'

If this had been Monica she'd have got on the blower and said, 'Pamela, come and sort this baby out.' But this wasn't Monica, and I wasn't Pamela. It was four of us, four frightened people.

When I'd burst through the door I'd had to stand for a long time just trying to make sense of what was happening. The small man was rushing about rearranging furniture and the woman was crouched down and howling. John was pulling down curtains and laying them on the carpet, and I thought he was going to bed in them. I couldn't figure out what was happening; I thought that the woman had been caught short. I thought they'd gone crazy, like they must have had a fight of some sort. Then I saw how the woman's face was screaming.

'Oh my God, she's having a baby, you'd better get on the phone for a doctor!'

The two men looked through me as though I was stupid, and John said, 'I could do with a coffee.'

'What?' I said, standing there, holding the door open.

'Put the radio on, get the shipping forecast.'

The shipping forecast? She's having a baby! Then I realised, the voice would help soothe her. 'Right,' I said, and turned to the radio. 'But we might have to wait for a while, yet.'

But John did not hear me, he was tearing my curtains up. I thought – 'Shit, I'll have to get blinds now.' 'What do you want me to do?' I said. They didn't hear me. I went into the kitchen to make coffee.

There is a mirror hanging over my sink unit and when I turned to it I almost shrieked. The man staring back at me was gaunt and quite deathly: his eyes burned, his lips were almost slobbering. 'Jesus Christ, this can't be me,' I thought. 'There can't be people tearing up my living room. There can't be a woman giving birth in it.'

I dashed back to the living-room and shouted from the doorway. 'This is ludicrous! She can't have the baby here, it's not healthy. You've got to let me phone for an ambulance!'

'I used to be a doctor,' said John.

'A doctor? You were a doctor?'

'Well, not a *qualified* doctor,' he said. 'But what difference does a piece of paper make? Get some water on. We need lots of water.'

'What for?'

'To bathe in. There'll be a mess and maybe blood.'

Oh Christ. The whole thing was getting out of hand now. I picked up the telephone but it suddenly went dead on me; the smaller man had ripped it from the wall socket.

'It's just you and us,' he said. 'It's just you and us. It's a baby, that's all you need to know about it.'

I went back into the living-room and saw that the woman was now on her back in a corner. She must have crawled there, seeking shelter. I went to her, tried to reassure her. 'It's going to be all right,' I said. 'John used to be a doctor. Just breathe slowly. I'm going to hold your hand for you.' And she grabbed my hand, and nearly broke it, her fingers squeezed pain through my knuckles. I looked for John, and he was pushing her legs apart. 'This is crazy, John. You've got to get help for this.'

'Have you got any water yet?'

'No, I haven't got water.' The woman squeezed on me, trying to make dust of me.

'It isn't going to be long, you know.'

I could have killed him. He was going to hurt her.

I started counting the way I did when I was a kid trying to hold back the nightmares. I read somewhere that if you'd started counting at the start of time, you still wouldn't have counted to a billion. I never believed that, and I tried to disprove it, in the darkness, counting up through the thousands. I wanted someone to come to me, to hold me until sleep arrived; but they didn't, although I often counted loudly. I knew they were wrong about it, I could count to a billion; but I never got there, never got to four thousand. That's what I started doing again, counting without any purpose. I did it for sanity, to hold back the darkness. I did it to defeat the nightmares.

'A hundred and ninety,' I said as John looked at me.

'Have you ever done this kind of thing before?' he said.

‘Of course I haven’t!’ The woman clung on to me. That’s my purpose, to help with her screaming. I am there to relieve all her agony.

‘We do appreciate it.’

‘I don’t believe it’s happening.’ But I did, though, because I kept counting. *Twenty four thousand.* (I cheated, to help me.) *Eleven thousand five hundred and twenty.*

‘I’m sorry about your phone,’ said the smaller man. (They seemed so much calmer than me, as if I had to deal with their panic.)

‘What’s happening?’ I whispered to him.

‘Nothing, it’s quietened down. I’m slipping off to make us some coffee.’

‘Oh, good.’ I changed my hands round so the woman could squeeze all the blood from the other one. Her grip was ferocious. I was given some inkling of the primeval fury which must lurk in the breast of a mother; a love she would die for, a love she would kill for; I wondered if that’s the last thought which passed through my wife’s mind as her car concertinaed to rubble. Her son would die with her, there was nothing to prevent it. She was helpless, she was already dying. Her fury would be boundless; the tree stump should have withered; but it didn’t, the car bypassed fury. I don’t think my wife died screaming with anguish, I think she died roaring with fury.

‘I had a son,’ I said, turning to the woman. ‘He was a good boy. I think you’d have liked him.’

The woman smiled; she seemed peaceful even though we had no shipping forecast. If I’d taped one, I could have played it back for her.

John had disappeared now, the room had grown quiet. The emergency appeared to have passed over us. ‘Is it not coming now?’ I said (ignorant in these matters).

‘I don’t know. I thought that it was.’

‘Well, never mind, I’ll still sit with you. Perhaps that was a preliminary warning.’

‘I’ve never had a child,’ she said.

‘I haven’t either. My wife handled that one. We must have some books somewhere that tell you what to do about it, but I don't know – ' (I remembered: I burned them.) 'I always got kind of squeamish about these things; I wasn't there when he was delivered. Hell of a kid though, he could have climbed mountains. There's no limit to what he could have accomplished.'

'Where is he now?' she said.

'Oh, he's – off with his mother somewhere; we don't talk much anymore.' I didn't tell her that we talked in the garden. When I'm out building heron traps (I lay intricate networks of wire round my pond) I explain what I'm doing to Matthew. He would appreciate it, he had quite an imaginative mind. (But the heron just picks its way through them.) I wish he'd come back to me, I'm sure that with his help I could fashion a trap that's impenetrable. I'd tell him about the shipping forecast. I'd get him a list of all the divisions so he could memorise them and never get lost in them. That way I'd protect him; he would always have something to cling to when life became lousy. I think that's why I play it for him, when I'm close to him during the darkness. I hope it brings comfort wherever he's roaming. I hope, that he's not really dead yet.

For a long time we lay saying nothing, waiting for something to happen. I could tell by the pressure which she never let ease on me, that something was probably imminent. But I wish we'd prepared for it; it all seemed last-minute. We didn't even take her in the bedroom.

'Have you got a name?' I said to her finally. 'I keep on calling you Theresa.'

'My real name is Pamela.' (Oh God, that's what Pam's called.) 'But I don't mind you calling me Theresa.'

I nodded. 'I have a friend called Malcolm J Barnett who wouldn't believe what's going on here. His whole life's a struggle to hang on to reason, but I have a feeling he's starting to lose it. I feel kind of sorry for him, there's nothing but conspiracies to undermine him and shake his 'normality'. He's got more fears than anyone I know; it's unkind really, he doesn't deserve it.'

'Why don't you tell him?'

'You can't talk to sane people.' I shrugged. 'He'd be too scared to listen.' I was just talking aimlessly, trying to take her mind off things in the lull which was preceding the tempest. I was trying to take *my* mind off them, I wasn't looking forward to them. I had the feeling that something bad might be happening. I wasn't even sure if this kind of thing is legal; God knows, I've enough things to cope with.

And soon after that events started in earnest, and for several hours there was nothing but screaming.

There is a law in this world which says some things are easy and some things are designed for catastrophe. We all have to bow to this, and no amount of good intention can alter the fact that at the end of the day the result was ordained in advance of us. Somebody, somewhere, makes these decisions for us. We struggle, but it's all a delusion. We have no real importance, nothing is subject to us. No one can live on our sayso. No one can choose the circumstances of their birth.

I've always felt rather sorry for the upper class: royalty, generals, old Etonians, colonels' daughters, those sort of people. I've always felt sorry for them because they're raised in the belief that they're superior to others, yet deep down they know they are not. They are merely people, not especially intelligent, not especially beautiful, not especially talented. Usually they are nothing but an accident of birth, though some of them rise above that awful start in life. It takes hard work and guts to spit out the silver spoon, to acknowledge that a Welsh miner, or a London bus driver, or a trawler fisherman, has ten times the life-spirit that they see in their family and friends – but one or two of them do it.

Most of them stay what they are though, and live on it the way an unborn chick lives on the yoke. They must know they're a hopeless breed (unless they're especially stupid) and it must give them a terrible complex. So on the outside they have this thin shell of superiority, and on the inside, a rather inferior yoke. This is why they're bluff and bluster and hide behind a ritual of etiquette and manners (and wealth). This is why they like the rest of us to call them 'sir' or 'lady' or 'm'lud' or 'your grace' – because this way they can keep their inferiority hidden behind barriers of titles. We do this to them. We call them these strange names because *we* like it too. Who would want to be associated with nothing people? If they *were* something, they wouldn't need the title, would they? Or the terrible accent? Or the cliques? Or each other's company? In the sixties they made an attempt to break free of their class bonds, but it didn't work because they couldn't find anything to do. So the majority of them still wait around for directorships to companies, or to be given a rank in the forces (was Lord Mountbatten ever destined to be anything but a viceroy or an admiral or a governor general - did he rise through the ranks and because of *exceptional ability* became first sea lord?) or spend/increase the family fortune. It's not much of a life for the poor sods. What sense of achievement do they get from being *given* everything? It's a shame because some of them are nice people and had they been born with coal dust in their mouths, might have made something of themselves. Instead most of them struggle all their lives in order to remain what they already are, which is usually just a comedy of manners stuffed with money.

Some of them achieve equality with ordinary people by being born dead. There's very little difference between an earl's son that leaves the womb lifeless, and a farm labourer's daughter who fails to draw the first breath.

Thus it was, after hours of intensity, that three men and a woman looked on a child which was born dead. We did all we could for it. We tried to be strong for it. We tried, but the child slipped away from us. It did not take that breath it needed, its heart did not pound with vitality. In short, it suspected that life was not meant for it. It died in its one chance at birth.

I suspect, looking back, there was little we could do for it, we toiled through the night with strange wisdom. A deep-rooted knowledge infused every one of us; we did things, because it was instinct.

Theresa was noble, she tried not to scare us, she tried to suppress all her screaming. I told her not to worry about it, we all wanted to scream, too. I have seldom seen women with such noble agony. It hurt me, it hurt me, too, physically. All of us encouraged her, we took turns at helping her; we bathed her, we soothed her, we yelled at her. We turned all the lights down, we turned them back up again, even the shipping forecast came out at full blast. (It's lucky that the neighbours are at least thirty yards away).

Bowls of hot water – (I know what they're for now) – and towels, and the spilled waters flowing. No sense of dignity, a sense of great purpose. And blood, and the soaked straw, and our wailing. Was this how the world began screaming and bloodied? Did we wail as we burst on the cosmos? And if we go out again will the last sound of humanity be the howl of a woman in childbirth? (I think that it might be; that primeval fury. If there's hope for us, I'm sure that it's female.)

But that did not aid us, those lifetimes of practice could not make a dead child start breathing. It came out quite slowly and I wiped all the mucus from it. I knew it was dead then, I knew it was futile; all that labour, it counted for nothing. Nor was it over, the child kept emerging; it came out, eventually, with a flourish. And John and I looked at each other, and someone had to tell her. But she knew, by our silence, her answer.

'It's dead, isn't it?' she said, and John could not answer her. And it was me who said, 'Yes. The child's stillborn.'

She wanted to hold it and John wanted to bury it, and for a long time I had to intervene with them. I held the baby while they battled over it, and after a while I took it away to the bedroom, and wrapped it in a pillow case and left it on the dressing table. I didn't know what else to do with it.

The room was in darkness, and I sat and prayed in it. Just me, and a wrapped-up dead baby.

The next morning, most of the signs of the birth had been cleared from the living-room. The straw had been swept up and much of the furniture had been put as it was before we started. *I* had not cleaned up, my arms were still covered in blood and dried mucus, and my clothes were a patchwork of stains. I went into the bathroom and was sick for a long time, and then spent a long time bathing. I passed all the morning there, afraid to come out again. (I was afraid that the squatters had left me.)

My house was disturbingly quiet. Nobody moved in it, and even the goat seemed to have abandoned its pitiful mewling. I appeared alone in it. I appeared more alone than I had been for a long time, as if I'd turned into a criminal. I don't know if it's criminal to help with a delivery, but it must be to conceal a dead baby; and I didn't know what we would do with it now. (Assuming the squatters had not left me.) Did we walk up to someone and say – 'Here's a dead baby'? Did we burn it, or – what did we do with it? All night I had hoped for some sign of existence from it, a movement, a murmur, a gurgling. But the sad heap of linen just lay like a bundle, a parcel, a consignment for hell. It had given me nightmares when I dozed in the early morning. Its image still haunted my vision.

I left the bathroom and padded about with a towel fastened loosely about me. No one had eaten yet, the kitchen was empty. I couldn't face my breakfast either. I sat in the living room with coffee and a cigarette, and the goat appeared, nuzzling my fingers. 'Hello boy,' I murmured, as though it was lonely (and I gave it all kinds of emotions). 'Is it just you and me now?' But the goat did not answer; it just started eating my bath-towel.

But we weren't alone. The French windows opened and Theresa limped in from the garden. It was bitterly cold out there, the wind whipped the apple trees, but all she had on was her birth smock. All the way from Siberia that wind came to lash at her; the wind has no sympathy at all. As in the *Great Hurricane* when it ripped off my roof tiles; it didn't care that this upset me.

Her feet were bare and covered with grass stains and mud and were glistening with water. Her hair streamed with moisture, her face was a death-mask, so white, so inhuman, so rigid. And yet she smiled at me, smiled as she dragged herself over the threshold and smiled as she slumped in the corner.

'How are you feeling?' I said, as shivers ran through her like echoes of last night's convulsions. I put a blanket round her shoulders and turned up the gas central heating.

'I'm okay,' she murmured. 'Still sore, but that's going now. I've just been out looking at the garden.'

'It's awfully cold out there,' I said. 'You ought to stay indoors. Would you like me to make you some breakfast?'

She shook her head and stared at the carpet. Her face had a look of confusion. 'I just – wanted to find some place to bury him.'

God. I stared at her. I hope no one saw this. She's going to plant a baby in my garden. But then, that seemed fitting, it was her own baby; surely she had the right to dispose of it? Didn't she? What would I have done when my own son was cremated? I didn't have the chance to consider it. Maybe I'd like to have him somewhere much closer to me, a place I could stand and watch over him. To plant a small garden for him, shield it with saplings, in the sunlight, where the sunlight could warm him. I would put a small pond by him with trickling water, a fountain, a pond of white lilies. I'd do anything for him to make him feel happy. (I'd make sure no herons disturbed him.)

My wife? I'm not sure. I don't think I could stand having her lying somewhere too close to me. It would make me go crazy to have her so close to me and I'd wonder if somehow I could 'preserve' her. I'd love just to talk to her, to be able to explain things, to say – 'This is why I am doing this.' Without her to talk to, I don't *know* why I'm doing things. I'm drifting. I'm nothing but driftwood.

I feel very low now, I'd like to pick up again. But, I don't know, I seem to have lost things.

'Where are the others?' I asked, suddenly looking at her.

'I don't know. Out walking.'

This day was a long one, it had no clear end to it; it drifted, as all of us drifted.

That night, as I lay on my bed looking for something that would help guide me into oblivion, my bedroom door opened and Theresa crept into the room, and rustled about in the darkness.

'What are you looking for?' I said, making myself sit up. 'What do you want of me? We've been through enough now.'

'I'm looking for my baby,' she whispered. 'I don't know where you've put him.'

I put the light on. 'It's better to leave him.'

'No,' she said, shaking her hair round her shoulders. 'I need to. We have to complete this.'

'Oh God,' I murmured, dragging the bedclothes off. There would never be an end to this madness.

Theresa was already dressed and I pulled on some clothes of my own. We were creeping about softly so as not to wake up the others (my clock said it was three in the morning) and we were creeping about almost silently so that judgement did not have to shine upon us (for in some things we're still very primitive). Theresa reached for the baby-parcel and I whispered at her to leave it.

'I want to hold him,' she said.

'Leave it, *I'll* hold him.'

'I want to.'

'Oh, for Christ's sake, you hold him.' I didn't want her to, but she was his mother. Or something; do dead things have mothers? I watched as she cradled him, though he must have been cold now. And I watched, but she did not uncover him. She looked almost beautiful, she must have prepared for this, putting clothes on I didn't know she had. And she must have washed her hair silently, inside the dark bathroom, and put on make-up by some pallid candlelight.

It was cold, I shivered, I pulled a warm jacket on. 'Are you ready?' Theresa just smiled at me. It wasn't a smile, I don't know what it was, really; acceptance, or some kind of mocking thing. If it was a smile, it was colder than the night air, it hurt me; it wasn't my idea, she forced me to do this.

We left the bedroom, picked our way through the living-room past two snoring bundles. The goat began following us, and I let it come with us; if I stopped it, it would probably start bleating. I opened the windows into the garden and put the exterior light on. The night was still blowing heavily, phantoms of rain danced and darted amongst the dark apple trees. We stepped out onto the wet grass; cold rain drove against us. I blinked at the south wind, and tried a quick prayer on it; but it mocked me, it just kept on coming.

I turned my back against it and trudged towards the garden shed, unlocked the stiff door and brought out some garden tools. I lit a storm lantern we once used for barbecues. (*We* once did, I no longer use it.) I shouldered the shovels, the pick and the garden fork and, holding the lamp out, moved forward.

'Where do you want to go?' I muttered.

'Into the woodland. I found a good place for him.' She didn't tell me where, so I just started walking; it's a small wood, it couldn't take that long.

We trudged through the darkness like two lonely pilgrims and the light from the house wall gave out on us, killed by the old, fallen garage. My feet sank into heavy mud but I pushed on, and we entered the woodland. The wind sang around us, the branches laid rain on us, a dark ancient holly loomed over us. ('Screw this for a lark,' I thought.) But I kept on walking, right round the woodland, hitting branches, dropping implements, growing desperate.

'Where do you want to go?' I cried. 'We've already walked round it twice!'

'Over there,' she said, pointing to a dead-bramble clearing. 'Over there. I want to clear out those brambles.'

I threw the tools down, and went to examine the site. It was a nice spot, except for the brambles. 'It will take us all night,' I said.

'It won't matter. Where would he go to?'

I began to rake at the ground, pulling out dead logs, ripping clinging ivy away from tree trunks. She held the lamp over me, then gently lay the baby down, and hung the lamp up and started to help me. We worked side by side, getting ripped by the same thorns, grabbing hold of the same concealed splinters. The baby somehow watched us; after a while I could see that, he was watching, to see where we put him. That made it important to make the site suitable, and I went back over the ground we had already cleared once. I picked every twig up, tore out every bramble, my hands screamed, my shoulders were bleeding. There was a sort of desperation about it after a while, to get the grave cleared before anyone saw us. We both started crying, our bodies were so weak for us, when we needed strength our bodies refused to help us.

The earth became churned up, it turned into mud on us; I clawed at it, dragging out great handfuls. Then I picked up a shovel and attacked the ground like a madman, gouging out root-balls, exhuming dead branches. I destroyed it, that dark clearing. I started to hack at it, slashing out crazily. Theresa stopped me. She said, 'It's all right now.'

I stared at her, panting – we were covered in mud now. 'How can it ever be all right?' I said. 'How can it ever be? We must make it perfect. We have to dig, until the whole place is perfect. Clear all these branches out, get the soil levelled out, clear out these roots so they won't grow again.'

But Theresa was smiling at me, kind of a sad affair, and she put her hand on my arm and said, 'No, it's all right now, we don't have to do any more. We'll rest for a while, then we can bury him.'

I looked over my shoulder at the pit we had dug for the child; it was tiny, but then he was so tiny. There wasn't much point in going on any further, we'd done everything we could for him.

I nodded. 'Okay,' I said, laying the spade down. 'We'll rest now. We'll have a cigarette.'

So we sat and smoked, in the rattling darkness, and cradled our flames from the downpour. And when the smoking was through, she put the bundle in the cold ground, and I watched while she sprinkled earth over it.

And we didn't say anything, no prayers nor commitments, and when it was over, we went back to the house in silence.

And the two men were waiting, awake and alert now. But they watched us, without saying anything.

DOG PEOPLE: THIRTEEN

The following day I called into the office, although this was not my original intention. I set off in the car with the idea of driving, trying to find something which would serve to distract me.

It was a quiet winter day with a grey sky looking over the world and a hard, bitter frost on the landscape. A day when the hoar-covered treestumps are like random tombstones scattered over the countryside by some maladroit giant. It was one of those days when the car took an age to warm up and my hands were like ice on the steering wheel; but this did not disturb me, I had no time to notice such things, I was far too wrapped up in my thoughts.

I set off, initially, in the direction of the sea wall, but the air was too cold to go walking. So I sat in the car trying to see over the sea wall, and thinking what a lonely spot I'd come to. Possibly the only company out here was grey herons, but they hid from me in the marsh reeds. They knew we were enemies and that if given license I would have hunted them down like the fish-killers they were. In search of some company, I switched on the radio, but that didn't do anything but bore me. I just sat there for an hour until I finally drove away again, and in the end I was simply driving around aimlessly. To tell you the truth I didn't know what I was doing, I had the feeling I could have driven like that for hours. But in the end even driving got to be fairly boring, there was nothing to look at but strangers. The strangers were okay, they had their own lives to distract them, but I could do nothing but drift on.

At times like that one can begin to appreciate what a small world it is we inhabit. There was no one to call on (no one that I wanted) only me, and I was tired of my company. I grew rather angry, I was self-pitying; I wished I had more to be proud of. I wasn't proud of anything for it seemed I'd achieved nothing, all I had was a facility for creating confusion. I confused my own colleagues, my friends, my own lifestyle. Like a battlefield I waited for carnage.

I smoked a lot of cigarettes and stopped for a coffee (I think it was in Hockley) and the car took me where it had a mind to. The world can be a vital place, full of activity, but the car took me to its more boring parts. I wanted to feel noble, like some overlooked poet, but it didn't happen, I merely felt rather foolish. It was a waste of a day to go driving around aimlessly; nobody would care if I died at it.

I guess I was uneasy about the burial of the baby, I wished it had not had to happen. I wished I could wake up and laugh off that nightmare, but some dreams are not works of fiction. We had buried a baby and I could not go back on it, there was no way I could dig the child up again. Christ, it had even ceased to seem like a child now, it was nothing but a bundle of bad luck. This time I thought I'd stepped out of normality. It scared me to feel so inhuman.

With no one to talk to, and no place to walk in, I wound up in the car park of the station. I caught the train to Liverpool Street and was glad that it travelled almost empty. It suited me to be wrapped up, contained in isolation. I rocked, like a man without meaning. It felt a long hour, though, a waste of some magnitude; though God knows what else I could do with it. And at the end of it I walked away like some kind of phantom. My whole life was vapid and vacuous.

In the office I didn't know what to do, I stood at my desk blankly staring at things. My colleagues were looking at me, uncertain and uneasy and I turned to look back at them. I made a paper hat out of a newspaper and put it sideways on my head.

'Napoleon,' I said.

Then gave it a quarter turn.

'Nelson.'

I wasn't trying to be funny. I don't know what I was trying to be. I wanted some attention I suppose, but at the same time I felt embarrassed and awkward, and wanted people to leave me alone, to get on with their own business. I don't know what I wanted, but it wasn't what I was getting. It was almost as if I were somebody else, someone very strange, someone unapproachable. No one took any notice. They just glanced sideways at each other and when one of the office juniors sniggered, somebody told him to shut up.

They began to annoy me. They were so obvious in their efforts to ignore me.

I think they were *afraid* of me.

I had nothing to say to them. My greatest surprise was that Malcolm J was still absent, his sickness must have been something terminal. We were both going through breakdowns (I'd figured at least this much out) but his must have been much worse than my own. I've always rather suspected that I was fodder for a breakdown, but for Malcolm it must have been something alien. I could accept it as an inevitable development, but for Malcolm his world must have blown up on him. I looked at his desk and it seemed rather pitiful, so lonely without his fat presence. The desk was a useless item without Malcolm before it, his papers would never be tended. Somehow I suspected that if Malcolm never came back his work would be left just to fester. No one would take it up, the office would adjust itself, it would bypass him, his clients would simply vanish. The office *was* Malcolm, was made a strange place without him; yet in his absence it mocked him and if a replacement was ever found for him, Malcolm's work would end up in a trash can. He'd be put in a filing room, 'Here lies Malcolm Barnett'. There would be no place available for him in the new world.

It struck me then, looking round the busy office, just how little we cared for the others, how little we would help them if they were in difficulty, or if their work was beginning to overwhelm them. We wouldn't say, 'Here, Malcolm, I'll help you with that one.' We would watch, with a grim fascination. We would take a strange pleasure out of watching him founder. If he burst into flames we would not call the Fire Brigade. Not from a sense of maliciousness, but plain curiosity. We would let him burn in order to see what it looked like. When Franklyn came in to see what was causing the smell, we would say, 'Barnett has spontaneously combusted,' and go back to what we were doing before. (Would Franklyn be shocked? Or would he be aggrieved that he had missed the show? Franklyn is predictably unpredictable).

We weren't a team we merely happened to work together. The work was our master and our colleagues were rivals, so we outgunned them, we cheated, we lied on them. Anything to make us seem better than they were, slightly wiser, a little smarter, more holy. We were all idle bastards who hoped to make graves of people, to dance on, to build on, to sneer upon. We'd look down on tombstones to say, 'I outlasted that bastard.' We would do nothing that would not promote us.

Poor Malcolm Barnett. Poor me. Every one of us.

It was on that cheerful note that I saw Franklyn.

He quietly stood and watched me for a while; for the first time he saw me with caution. I guess I looked a little unusual, unshaven, dishevelled, uncaring. He didn't storm up to me, I think he had compassion. For the first time he saw we were mortal.

'Hello Steven,' he said.

'Bernard.' I nodded. (It was the first time I'd ever called him Bernard).

'There's a lot on your desk,' he said, trying to sound helpful, but it was clear he was not too concerned about it. It was me who was worrying him, it was me that he cared for. Good old Bernard, he quite likes me after all.

'I was going to have a coffee,' he said. 'Would you like to come and join me?' And I nodded, and shrugged, and walked after him.

We sat in his office where his cacti still irritated me and where once, in my dreams, I put an end to him. I rammed his brass letter-opener clear through his eyeball, and he died with a lot of dumb screaming. But not on this occasion. I wasn't going to hurt him. I needed him, needed someone to talk to.

'You're looking tired,' he said.

'I'm feeling tired. I was up all night burying a baby.'

If any proof were needed I had promptly volunteered it: I was clearly undergoing a breakdown. Franklyn appreciated this, he knew about breakdown. Franklyn knew something about everything. He didn't pursue it because it was clearly a crazy comment, but he wanted to do something to help me.

'Is the work getting on top of you?' he asked.

'The squatters are getting on top of me. It was a game at first, now I'm not so sure of it.'

'Which squatters are these?'

'The ones in my living-room.'

Franklyn nodded. 'How long have they been there?'

'About seven weeks, now. I don't think I'll ever get rid of them.'

'Do you want to get rid of them?'

'I'd like to go back a bit. I'd like to go back to the beginning. What's really bothering me is that I'm starting to get angry with them, and I'm frightened I might want to kill them. I've got a gun at home, I used it for skeet shooting, I'm worried that I might blow their brains out. When you get to think of things like that, you worry that you might make it happen. It might be like some kind of voodoo. I don't want to kill them, that would be a big mistake. But I'm worried. They're starting to irritate me.'

'Have you talked to your doctor?'

'I'd rather give the gun away. But if I did, then I would be defenceless.'

We stared at each other. This was unkind to Franklyn, but I didn't know what else to do then. It wasn't his problem that I was going crazy, but on the other hand, what else was he there for? He must owe me something for all my unhappiness. He'd helped it. He'd not made me cheerful.

'Is there any way I can help you at all?'

Poor Franklyn. 'I don't really think so. Some things, you can't make them happen. What I'd really like to do, what I want to happen, is that I wake up one morning and my wife is back with me, and my son, and there's nothing gone wrong with us. There wasn't an accident, they didn't get cremated, they were hiding for some reason, and now they've come back to me. This is the one thing that I want to happen. And it won't, and I fear I can't cope with it.'

Franklyn stared at me, lost for suggestions. The answers were too plain to utter. 'You really ought to get some help,' he said. 'Someone you can talk to. Professional help.'

'I don't want to talk about it,' I said, turning away from him. 'I just want to grieve over it. I haven't been doing that yet. I tried to forget it and that was a mistake really. It festered, it built up like cancer. And now that it's ready to come out in the open, I don't know if I can prevent it.'

'It's not good for you to be like this,' said Franklyn.

'I know that.' I nodded. 'I know lots of things, but they don't count for much now. I'm dying. It's hurting inside me.'

'You're not dying,' he said. 'And Angela wouldn't like to see you like this. She wouldn't like to see you make yourself unhappy.'

He remembered my wife's name! Businessmen are good at that. They practise remembering names and asking after children, to impress their clients, make them feel special. But there was no reason why he had to remember Angela. He had only met her once. I think. At the firm's dance. Maybe she had made an impression on him? Angela was a striking woman.

'She can't see me at all, though,' I said, rather cruelly. And I stood up. 'I think I might leave now.'

'You don't want your coffee?'

'I don't think I want anything.' And I walked away past all his cacti.

'What about Adams?'

'I'll try to have a look at it.' But I didn't, I just left the office.

I didn't go home, though, I walked round London, like a stray dog I went where life took me. I walked from the business centre down to the docklands, and a cold lonely sky came along with me. The sky was watching me, but I didn't want to stare back at it for too long in case I saw something. Faces, or something even worse.

It was cold when the night came, ruffling my dog hair. I shivered, and thought about howling. My squatters were dog people, they slunk around me, but me, I was built for the wastelands. I started to prowl, but the streets were not meant for me. We have territories and this did not belong to me. I wanted a moon smiling down like Malcolm Barnett, something solid, a light I could hold to. But I could find nothing, a dark sky and city lights. A man's world, where dogs are not welcome.

And I don't want to be a dog. They're subservient and I want to be vital. I want to get back in control. I still have humanity coursing inside me. (All this, and I still bury babies).

I looked for a station and caught a train homewards, though it was midnight when I finally arrived there. Suddenly I realised I had lost all the fear that had been in me for most of the day. I really hadn't understood my feelings until now. I hadn't known I was afraid, a sort of unknown terror in me, until it left me. Now it had gone, I knew what it had been. Had it gone? Maybe this was another unknown state of fear which would be revealed to me only by its absence? Maybe there are layers of terror that peel away and with each new one we say, 'Thank God that's over. Now I can relax.' But we never can relax because there's always another skin holding in fear like sausage meat that will spill out and empty us completely once the last one had gone. Maybe we're full of nothing *but* fear? Seven epidermises containing nothing but layers of dark mushy terror.

Did it make any sense when I finally got home again? I don't think so. Not really, I don't think so. Somehow I knew that I must be going crazy, and had been going crazy for a long time. Yet at the same time I still thought myself perfectly normal, I could believe both of these states were within me. I was crazy and I was sane. They didn't seem to contradict one another. They managed to exist side by side in the same mind. It crossed my thoughts that perhaps the dog people, the squatters, didn't even exist; that I'd made them up to help me go round the bend. I'd have to ask them if they were real, maybe the next time I saw them. I stood for a while in the garden and saw that a light was coming out of the woodland, a warm light, the light of my lantern. Someone was up there, lurking in my woodland, hanging about near to the grave-site.

I crept up there through brambles, through mud, through the dead grass. I watched, and I saw the child's mother. Theresa was there, she stood at the graveside, she murmured and her breath was a storm-cloud. That proved she existed. Imaginary figures don't breathe.

I stood for an hour watching her grieving. She had lost him, no prayers could repair that. With a sick heart I went to my own grave, my own house, the home I had cursed with my memories. I should have abandoned it. We built it together, my wife and I, it had no use now. I wanted to leave it, but what did I change it for? A stray life? A dog slowly wandering?

'Where's the goat?' I said, looking at John, who was watching me.

'We killed it. We had to do something.'

'What do you mean 'You had to do something'? Where's the goat, man? For God's sake, the goat I said!'

'We had to kill it, I couldn't stand seeing it; with my son dead, I couldn't stand seeing it.'

'You killed the flaming goat?' I said.

'We had to. I had to repair things.'

'By killing a goat?' I cried. 'You killed a goat because your son died? What on earth did the goat have to do with your son dying? It wasn't the goat's fault, it won't bring him back again.'

John shrugged and turned away from me. 'It was necessary. I needed to do it.'

'You bastard,' I yelled at him. 'What kind of thing is that? A religion or something? You sacrifice *goats*? Who do you think you are? Abraham? Killing a goat won't bring your son back. What happened was that Abraham was *told* to sacrifice Isaac, but he didn't have to – *then* he killed the goat...'

'We're not interested in that,' said John. 'I don't know those people. I never met them.'

I couldn't believe it. The only thing that I *liked* was the goat, and they'd killed it, in some kind of ritual. 'How did you do it?' I asked him.

'I strangled it. It's out in the garden.'

Jesus Christ. I went almost blind. They'd killed it for no stupid reason.

'You're so stupid!' I shouted at him. 'You're worse than two children. You killed it, because you were angry!'

'So what?' he said, and Michael joined in with him.

'It had to go. It was essential.'

'Essential my arse!' I said. 'I hate you, you're so bloody stupid!' There were tears in my eyes and a furnace inside me. 'I liked it! For God's sake, I liked it!'

'Well it's dead now,' said John.

'After all I've done for you!' I cried. 'I took you in, I helped to look after you, I fed you, for Christ's sake I even helped to bury the baby! I've done all I can for you, I turned my house over to you. You repay me by killing an animal!'

'We didn't ask you to take us in,' said John. 'You welcomed us, you wanted to help us.'

'Because I thought you were decent! Because I felt sorry for you. But you're not decent, you're nothing but goat killers.'

'So that's all it was?' said John. 'You merely felt sorry for us? We were stray dogs, and you helped look after us.'

I glared at him, then I ran past him, the rage still in the forge. There was something inside my head which felt white-hot. It felt as if it was going to explode at any second. I bounded up the staircase.

At the top of the stairs I wrenched open a cupboard and took out my old sporting shotgun. It was stiff from disuse and through not enough cleaning, but I broke it by pounding the barrels. I pulled it until the lock clicked into place and looked down the sheer metal slideways. I searched through the cupboard for cartridges. They weren't there, I kept them somewhere else, I couldn't remember where I put them. I ran through the rooms opening cupboards and drawers, and found them at the back of my desk-drawer. A blue box of cartridges, half of them gone now, their shot scattered randomly over the cold Essex marshes the night after my wife and son died. But twelve still remained for me, small tubes of death. I grabbed them. I pushed two of them into the barrels.

Then the gun clicked into place and I ran back to face John and Michael.

'You bastards!'

I brandished the gun at them, laughing as they bolted.

'Yeah, go running!' I yelled. 'I bet the goat tried to run!' But I didn't fire at them. I ran out to the garden and aimed the gun at the lawn and pulled on both triggers. They must have heard the sound in hell. It grooved a hollow out of the night. Bits of stone and turf flew everywhere, and I felt somehow elated.

'That's it!' I yelled, looking up at the darkness. 'That's it! It is really all over now!'

I ran back into the house and, swinging the gun by its barrels smashed the stock against a wall and in a small cloud of plaster it broke in my hands and I threw the useless halves at the window.

Then I galloped upstairs to the cupboard where my suitcases lie and I pulled one out and dashed to the bedroom. I stuffed some clothes in it, all I could think of, and my shaver, my hairdryer, medicines. I grabbed a sleeping bag from under the bed and charged out to a night which was raining.

'You can have it!' I called to them. 'It's finished. I'm leaving! I hope you rot in it. Do what you want with it.' I ran down the path and clattered out on the dark lane, then thought 'Sod it!' and went back for the Sigma. God Almighty, I'd given them my own home, damned if I was going to leave them my car as well.

I bundled inside it and hauled all my luggage in, and with a squeal of black tyres I roared out of there.

To hell with them all, it was me and the darkness, me and the cold crazy darkness. Burying babies. It had all gone too far now, even if it might prove unreal. I had to leave my madness behind in the house. It seemed the most sensible thing to do, run away. I wondered why I hadn't thought of running before. It seemed the answer to all my problems, surely you can't go mad just *anywhere*: there are special places for that sort of thing. Home. Friends' houses. The hospital. Places like that. If you feel yourself going round the bend, the best thing to do is run away from it. Leave it all behind. In the streets everyone is divorced from reality. Insanity is the norm there. I was running to the place where sane people are unusual and therefore out of place. Where sane people are regarded with suspicion and considered dangerous. I was running away to those who were like myself. As one of the street people, I would be normal.

There had to be some place where I fitted in, without having to forcibly change myself.

DOG PEOPLE: FOURTEEN

Malcolm J Barnett looked at me horrified; every nightmare he'd ever had had come home to him. 'What?' he said, in what was almost a whisper. 'What did you say? I didn't hear you.'

I said, 'I need a bed for the night. I've left home. I need a place to sleep tonight.'

'Jesus Christ,' he whispered, 'don't say that to me. How can you leave home? It's your house. You're the only one who lives in it!'

'Not any more,' I said. 'The squatters took over it. I'm lonely, I need a long sleep somewhere.'

'*Here?*' he said, wildly. 'You want a bed in this house? This is *my* house, for God's sake, I live here.'

'I know,' I said (we were talking on his doorstep). 'I just want a bed for a night or two.'

'*I* can't give you a bed,' he said. 'Jesus Christ, the kids are asleep. What are you doing here? You're driving me crazy, I don't want to know about this. Why are you doing this to me, Steven?'

Poor Malcolm Barnett, he really looked rough now, his breakdown was taking its toll of him. Two men in breakdowns, on a dark rainswept doorstep. What would the neighbourhood think?

I looked at him carefully, following the course of it, the way it had mussed up his hairstyle and darkened his jaw-line, had made all his clothes fall away from him. He was standing in bare feet, his toes cold and lonely, his fingernails bleeding from chewing. 'Oh Jesus, Malcolm,' I said to him slowly. 'Why did you let yourself go like this?'

'What do you mean?' he said, stammering, taking a step back from me. 'There's nothing wrong with me. Not like you're suggesting. I'm just having a bit of matrimonial trouble. Nothing else. It'll get sorted out. She would never leave the children.'

'No, I know,' I sighed, and I wanted to hold on to him, to reassure him, to make him less lonely. But he wouldn't take that, he'd not understand me; I'd frighten him, he had enough wrong with him. 'Jesus, Malcolm, I'm sorry it came like this. It's the real world, it's hard to exist in.'

'What do you mean?' he said, and he might have been crying, or it might have been me trying to read too much. Maybe Malcolm never cries. Maybe that's why he wound up this way.

'You look cold, mate,' I offered. 'You want to put some shoes on. You'll freeze to death, you need to look after yourself.'

He looked at his feet. 'I'm not having you here,' he said. 'I've – I've got domestic problems at the moment. My wife – . You're not staying at my house. Go to Franklyn's house, he practically loves you.' He paused, then said, 'Why are you wearing that silly hat? It's a hamburger box, isn't it?'

I nodded. 'You might not have noticed in your state, Malcolm, but it's raining. I have to protect my head. Anyway, you're right, Malcolm, I'm sorry I came here. I didn't know where else I could go.'

'You're not coming in,' he said. 'You're not coming to my house. It's midnight, in fact, it's after midnight.'

'The world doesn't stop, Malcolm,' I murmured.

'It's gone *midnight*!' He seemed to be pleading with me. 'My wife's not home yet...' He peered over my shoulder, out into the rainy gloom, his eyes moody. 'She's probably missed her bus, I expect. I don't even know his name. Her children are asleep in there and where the hell *is* she? You would think she would be concerned about the children at least.'

'It's midnight. It doesn't really matter.' I sighed. I stared along his empty street and looked at the lights in the houses. Plenty of lights in there, but no one to help me. I needed him. I needed Malcolm Barnett.

I needed nobody but what they could offer, their comfort, compassion, a bed I could sleep in, some bare recognition of the plight I was lost in, a kind word, a moment, a touch on the shoulder, a candle to burn through this darkness. So many people around me, so many hallways – I've stood in doors, I've heard their calling, warm and soft and filled with laughter, but nobody asks me in further. Waiting in doorways (collecting for charities, I took round petitions about nuclear weapons) and no one said, 'You look so cold out there. Why don't you come in by the fire for a while?'

'Can I come in by the fire?' I asked Malcolm Barnett.

'Of course not, we're going to bed soon – when she comes in. Find a hotel somewhere, go back to your own house; we don't need this kind of behaviour.' And by 'behaviour' he suggested I was playing around with it, and couldn't see how much I was suffering.

I was silent. I stayed on the doorstep looking down *Bromley Gardens* and shivered, felt bleak, seemed abandoned. I had no place to go to, no one I could talk to, no one who did not need explanations. Such a big world, such a tiny lost soul in it. Why didn't he help me? Did he think I was fooling?

'I've got a tent,' he said at last.

'A tent?'

'There's a tent in the out-house. We've never used it much, you can take it if you need it. You might find a place you can put it.'

'A tent,' I said bleakly.

'It's all I can offer.'

'I'll take it.' Why not? I was desperate.

'I'll go and fetch it. Hang on there a minute.' And he pushed the door until it closed on me.

Two hours later, having sat in a car park a while, I returned to the dark Bromley Gardens. Most of the lights were gone now, the residents were asleep; not a flicker of life came from Malcolm's house.

I parked down the street a way, took the tent from the Sigma and, in the darkness, set the tent up on his front lawn. I pushed my old sleeping bag in, curled up in its cold kiss, and shivered, and slept from exhaustion.

No one disturbed me, no one interrupted me. I slept fitfully, not far from Malcolm. He wasn't aware of me. I hoped he'd take pity on me. I still hoped that he'd ask me inside.

In the morning cars made their way to the station and their engines called me from oblivion. I lay in a grey haze as breath snaked out of me. I thought, if I lay here, I'm unharmed.

At about nine o'clock I looked out of the tent-flap and saw a night's drizzle cold around me. The houses looked washed-out, forlorn and dejected. Without lights, they looked quite unwelcoming. I looked at Malcolm's house and he was standing looking back at me, at a window, the lace curtain pulled aside. He made no harsh gesture to me, called out no greeting; he didn't have to, I could see what he was thinking. I was making him unhappy, that was all I was doing to him. I hurt him, somehow abused him.

I'm sorry, Malcolm, I didn't intend this. I packed up and left without turning.

There's no place for Malcolm (trapped by his lace curtains) and no place for me to demand things.

Then again, maybe he wasn't looking at me. Maybe he was looking for someone else.

I didn't know what to do again. I wandered round for several hours then made my way back to my office. I had vague thoughts of staying there (though why, when I hated the place?) and I wondered if Franklyn would let me. Or perhaps I need not ask him that, just hide until the building was empty. I could at least get cleaned up in there, take tea and biscuits, could sleep on a bed made of folders. Or sleep in the first aid room, overdose on lint bandages, die there, make Franklyn take pity on me. Except he wouldn't take pity, he'd just get pissed off with me. They'd laugh at me. Underneath, they would laugh at me.

It wasn't a very good idea, I surely had more guts than that in me. Yeah, I'm not going to go down simply whimpering, just pleading; I'm a strong man, I have lots to offer yet. I didn't come this far to die in a sick-room. I've still got ideas yet. To prove it I took Felix Adams's folder and went into one of the interview rooms where we go when we need to work quietly. I took all the pages out, made a neat pile of them, then burned them in one of the waste bins. One after the other I let them blaze golden, to ashes, to flecks of black mystery. Let them sort that one out (I knew there were no copies). It would take them forever to rebuild it. They'd never catch Adams (though he's guilty as hell, I worked that one out a long time ago) or his widow. It would keep someone happy, being choked on this childishness, but, for God's sake, we all work at something. Give someone overtime, shake Franklyn's attitude. In some ways, it was the best thing I did there.

As an afterthought I took the fast food wrapper off my head and set fire to that too. It had offended Malcolm. Then I walked away, my bridges burned. No future. No past to ignore me.

Truly free now, and emboldened, I walked out to start a new life for myself.

DOG PEOPLE: FIFTEEN

'Monica?'

'Steven? Where are you?'

'I'm in Manchester.'

'Manchester? What are you doing there?'

'I'm squatting.'

The silence which followed told me that Monica believed me.

I could picture what she was doing, down the phone line, two hundred miles away. She would be moving from the kitchen to the lounge with her portable phone; sitting at the glass-topped table (with a view over her formal garden); maybe she'd reach for a cigarette. She would pick up the ebony table-top lighter, stroke a flame from it, let smoke curl and writhe past her features. She would lay the cigarette in the ashtray. She would frown at me.

'Are you okay?'

'Yes, I think so. Mostly I'm okay. I think that I'm okay.'

(A pause.) 'How are you living?'

'Kind of – carefree.'

'You mean you're without worries?'

'No, not exactly that way. I mean, I don't have any responsibilities.'

'Are you happy?' (She paused again, breathing her cigarette).

'I think so. I don't know. I might be.'

'You're very worrying, Steven, we've all been concerned about you.'

'All of you?'

'I have. I'm worried.'

'You don't have to be,' I said (I talk more slowly these past weeks). 'You don't need to. There's nothing much wrong with me.' (Another long silence. We're good at long silences. It used to be, we had to keep talking all the time. I'm happier, this way, with silences.)

'Would you like to come home again?'

'I don't think so. I may do, but not at this moment. I've got things to do; I don't know what they are yet. When I do them, I may want to come home again.'

'How are you surviving? Have you got any money with you?'

'Money? I haven't got money.' I stared at a man who was watching the phone box; he's a mad-man, he can't quite believe this. He believes there are more of me, occupying the phone box; he's counting, he thinks he sees – twelve of me. This is something of a mystery to him and he can't quite accept it. He counts me again, to make certain. Two hands of fingers, plus two extra fingers. He counts me, then moves away frowning. What do you call that? Is the man schizophrenic? I don't know. (He counts something else now).

'Are you still there, Steven?'

'Yes, I'm still listening.'

'I said, what are you doing about money?'

I stare into the distance. Not a great deal, really. I steal it, or, maybe, I bum it. Yes, I think I've tried begging but I'm not very good at it. They pass me before I approach them. Other men who look much less capable than I do seem incredibly successful at begging. I guess they've got confidence and I've not achieved that. It goes a long way does some confidence.

'I'm using my credit card,' I said. 'They haven't caught up with me. I'm way over the limit but – I'm lost to them. I use it for food – I can't get money with it – at the moment, they can't catch up with me. It's rather amusing, really, I just keep on buying things with it, I buy things, and I don't even need them. I bought a new watch yesterday and left it on a park bench. But it doesn't matter, I didn't really need it.'

'Give me the account number,' Monica said. 'I'll pay in some money to your account.'

'That's very kind of you.'

'It's not kind. I love you. I'm very concerned about you.'

'I love you, too. I'm sorry if it's upsetting you. But, really, there's nothing much wrong with me.'

'What's happening about the house?'

'The house? The squatters are living in it.'

'Are they paying for it?'

'Paying for it? I shouldn't think so.'

'Well I'd better put some money in, to cover the mortgage.'

'You're very kind really.' And I meant it. I meant it so much that I started to cry a little. I cried, though I wasn't unhappy.

'How did you get there?'

'To Manchester? I drove here. I came up to stay with my mother. But it didn't work out, I don't like her new husband. It's awkward, to sit there in silence. I don't know what to say to him, I try but – we just look at each other. It's awkward for him, I think, also. The first night I was there I could hear them make love together, it must have been my presence caused it. I think he wanted to prove something, but it's weird to have your mother, who is sixty, getting bonked in the next room to you. I wanted to say, 'Mother, for Christ's sake keep it down in there.' But it's sad, really. I didn't like it there.

'Would you believe, I actually slept under a railway bridge at one time, like a vagrant? I had my own carton. The first night was weird, I was the only one under there, and I just had my sleeping bag, without any cardboard. I was sitting hunched up under an advert for Heineken, and a dog came up and started to sniff at me. It was just a mongrel, a throwback, some kind of primeval dog, a brown cur, a dog with no breeding. I thought I'd make friends with it, but really it was far removed from that. It was savage, and wanton, and dangerous. I could see it was dangerous because its eyes kept on weeping, and really, a dog shouldn't cry much. So I thought, 'Those aren't tears because it's lonely. Those tears are its anger.' So I was wary of it then, and I didn't make a move for a while, and I thought, maybe I can startle it and scare it. If I jumped at it suddenly it might run away from me. I think, that it wanted the space I was in.

'But as I was thinking this, before I got around to it, a whole pack of dogs turned a corner on me. There must have been – thirty of them, and I thought, 'My God, these dogs take the city over at night.' There are dogs everywhere, you know, they're walking all over the place. They feed off the city. Who knows what kind of damage they might cause? And I thought, 'God, they're like people, they've got the same expressions.' And maybe they're meant for that, to feed on us, to parasitise us, to take it from us, and one day to rule us. At night, in the darkness, while the world's asleep. And, in the daytime, they might become businessmen. Do you ever get thoughts like that? I've been thinking about it a lot lately. About people who really look dog-like.'

Monica was silent for a time, and then she said, 'I don't really think of things like that.'

I said, 'I didn't. But now I'm not sure any more.'

'Why don't you come home, Steven?'

'Home is where the heart is.'

'Where is your heart now?'

I don't know, really.

The dogs: I didn't finish talking about the dogs, the way they stood around me like museum visitors and I was some statue of old days. Mangy curs, no social graces between them, old war wounds, old broken-down jaw-lines, odd angles, unloved sores, broken teeth, torn-out notches, loose ears, wild eyes, snake-cunning. 'Get away you bastards,' I said. 'You flea-bags, you dirty mongrels. Push off.' But they didn't push off, they were watching me. Maybe I was one of them, hunched up in my sleeping bag; a new dog, new face, an old hunter. They wanted the food I had, two grubby sandwiches. 'It's my food, I need it, I'm hungry.'

But so were they hungry, they must always be hungry, in the jungle, at night, in the dark streets. 'Can't you pick on someone else? It's my supper, I'm saving them.' The biggest dog started to snarl at me. It was bigger than I was, it stared down its snout at me, its dark eyes were cruel and superior. 'You're out of your depth, man,' it must have been thinking.

'For God's sake, I've been through enough, you know. Don't we have anything in common? Can't you see that? I'm an outcast, I'm just like the rest of you.' But I wasn't. I was human, these dogs were the masters. I threw the sandwiches to them and they leapt on them, fighting like hoodlums. The sound of their snarling rang out through the archway.

I really couldn't take it, these Manchester hoodlums. I spent the rest of that night in a phone box. Not the same phone box from which I called Monica but, still, there were many similarities. I moved on at daylight (as, now, it was evening when I hung up and said my goodbye to her). Now things were different, I had a home to go to. And finances. Monica would help me there.

I walked through the streets a while watching all the people who still seemed to think they'd a place in the world. Rushing about their business, important, enslaved by it, enraptured, engrossed, oh so street-wise. I wasn't like that, I knew my limitations. They were false fools, but I, I was clear now.

The squat I was living in (if it could be called living) was a large terraced house in north Manchester. It looked like a normal house, like normal folk lived there, but inside, you could see it was a camp-site. There was no normal furniture inside, no regular heating supply; a cold house, a damp house, a cave, really. I lived on the second floor in a boarded up bedroom.

It was ten o'clock when I returned home that night and I fell over something in the yard. We don't use the front door, but the back's always open; it's a free squat, anyone could walk in on us. I think it was a bicycle which nearly broke my ankle, and I was bleeding as I limped through the kitchen. We don't use the kitchen, much, it's just for flushing food away and, really, one wouldn't like to eat in there. Beyond the dark kitchen you come to a hallway where all kinds of things are collected: old books and magazines, old clapped-out record players; it's a junk yard, one day we hope to make use of it. One day. We have lots of plans for a mythical 'one day' but none of us take them too seriously.

Then there's the staircase which leads to the bedrooms, and perched on the staircase was Mary. Mary doesn't own any of us, she has no claim to us, but she likes to be informed what we're up to. She's very demanding, really, with positive nosiness. She does own us, somehow. I think so.

'Where have you been?' she said.

'I was making a phone call.'

'A phone call? Good God, you're a businessman then. Did you get any deals going, make any contacts to get rid of that stuff in the hallway? We could do with getting rid of it, it's starting to clutter the place up.'

'It was just a phone call,' I said, and sat down with her. I was a few steps below her and I passed up a cigarette and she sniffed at it as if I might poison her.

'I've been sitting here for hours,' she said. 'I was waiting to see how many people passed me.'

'How many did?' I asked.

'No one. They all ignored me.'

I looked away from her, smoking, letting my hands dangle over the sharp peaks that my knees made. Mary is twenty-six, quite a bit younger than I am, but she talks to me as if she was older. An ugly girl (I'm not mistaken) with bad teeth and bad breath and poor skin and lost hair, she works, now and again, on the pub scene. She picks up crazy men who think her sex is worth something, usually she also knocks them out with a lump of wood, and that way she makes sure she's paid enough. One day she came home with a thousand quid in her pocket (some navvy on his way back to Ireland). We managed a party before the shops closed on us that night, but the next day she managed to lose it all. She's rather stupid, really. She can't hold on to things. (I should talk.) In some ways, I can't criticise her. I think she'll survive, really, life won't creep up on her. Some people look almost endless.

'What were you doing?' she said.

'I said. I was making a phone call.'

'Oh yeah. A phone call. I've got no one I could call.'

'Your family,' I offered. 'Why don't you call your family up?'

'What fucking good would that do?'

We dropped it; we have a lot of conversation like that here. I think that it's practice for when we're out in the real world; you can't be an outcast without arguing.

Mary wants to make love with me. She always wants this thing. And one day I might have to agree with her. I can't pay her any money but she's often not concerned with that; it's the lump of wood she uses which worries me. I said to her once, 'You won't slug me afterwards?' And she said, 'Of course not.' But how much can I trust her? I don't want her going crazy on me and beating my brains out, but on the other hand, I would like to make love with her. There's something about women like her that makes me attracted to them; it's almost, that their ugliness makes them superior. They can't try enticing you, it would be a grotesque parody, so it must be something within them, a power that a pretty woman lacks. Maybe they're good at it without those pretensions, those superficial gimcracks like beautiful blue eyes and cupid bow lips and curves. There's something about the grotesque that attracts me.

'Where would we do it?' I said.

'What?' She said, frowning at me.

'Have sex?'

'I don't want to have sex with you!' Now she's glaring at me as if I'm an idiot. I don't know, I'm not good at guessing things. Maybe she doesn't want me, maybe she wants me crawling to her. I don't know, could I go through with crawling?

Probably.

'I'm not crawling.'

'I never said I wanted you to.'

We drop that subject and go on to the weather forecast which says we're going to be in for a cold snap. If we have a bad cold snap we're all going to freeze to death here. We talk about ways to get around it. They're mostly impossible ways, like setting fire to the house. I think that we'll have to sleep together. Jesus, I don't think I want to sleep together, there are seven in this house and they hate me. Well they don't all hate me, but some of them do, they don't trust me because I'm not good at this. I've not been taught squatting (in my house I looked after them). My talents are not very practical. I think that they actually view me as a parasite; I'm a parasite existing on squatters. How low can one get? I wouldn't like sleeping with them, and I bet I'm the cold one; I bet I'm the one on the outside. I'd like to sleep with Mary and crawl right inside her, but I'd probably get shaken out in some alleyway. Get beaten to death with a stick. Maybe just come out dead? God, that poor baby lying out in the cold ground. I might go back in spring and plant some flowers for him.

'We'll just have to wrap up in plenty of blankets,' said Mary.

'I suppose so.'

I might go to a hotel.

DOG PEOPLE: SIXTEEN

There is a certain amount of tension between the residents of the squat. I imagine this is not uncommon amongst animals which have no pecking order, and in the squat we have none, for none of is dependent upon the others. We have dependency for certain things, security, comfort, but there are no bonds between us. For this reason, the animosity, I know I shall not be a dweller here for too long, I'll move on, I will drift, I'll seek friendship. If it is true that I've cracked up, the rift has no magnitude and, inside, I'm still the same person. I'm just taking a breather from life's constant harrying, I'm waiting, I'm searching for something. (Or I am now deluded. I recognise all these possibilities, I have time now, nobody depends on me.) I retreat, but I do not take flight. And I watch, but I've still time to listen.

However, the insecurity and relative intensity of the squat is depressing. There is constant haggling over meaningless details, the noises, the smells we make, the ways we contribute, what we take and what we sometimes steal from it. I have stolen blankets and I have no intention of returning them, not unless I'm driven to it. I'm much harder already. I'll trample to get food, I'll hold on, I'll spit like a vixen. The bastards, they're not coming into my room, I make sure of that by sealing up the hole in the wall. There's quite an intricate array of locking devices, which I inherited.

And then again, it's fun. We get drunk and fall around a lot, and have parties and music and dance with each other (or dance alone) and there are no inhibitions and certainly no vanity and one thing we're free from is avarice. The only one who ever comes in with any money is Mary, and she's very free with it and usually loses it. We have good times; it's not all despairing. It's better than the squatters my house had. Jesus Christ, I ended up giving it to them! We've got no ties at all here: if it burns down we move on, we split up, we live hard. No one to cling to us, no one to mourn for us, there's no one who, really, gives a damn for us. And what a blessed freedom that is.

The only one I truly like is Mary, who takes it upon herself to dominate us, but I don't honestly mind that because I've never been dominated and, deep inside, I don't think she means it. It's just a small game for her (she cries if you snap at her). She's a young dog with ambitions, she's not a pack leader.

I've spent a lot of time talking to her, stroking her ankles, listening to tales of her wandering travels. Mary has no direction in life, she follows the rain around, she finds things then throws them away again. I don't think she's a happy girl but she's certainly not as unhappy as someone like, say, Malcolm J. He is a truly unhappy person and will never be otherwise, for he attempts so hard what's not designed for him. Malcolm's a teddy bear, he can't be a yuppie, but he devotes his whole life to it. It's such a sad waste really, no wonder he cracked up. Poor Malcolm, poor unwanted teddy. I talk about many things I can't talk about with Malcolm, and Mary understands every one of them.

She calls me the *Doctor*, she thinks that I'm brainy, but she is much wiser than I am. I'd like to take her home with me, but she would just wander away again. I'd like to marry her, but she doesn't love me.

One evening we went to the cinema together on the strength of a drunk she'd just laid out. It was no kind of film really, mad things and mayhem but for a long time she sat holding hands with me. In the relative dark of a cinema auditorium, with your hand held, your fingers rubbed softly, you forget that the woman sitting next to you isn't the most beautiful person in the world. And I suppose if I'd kissed her, with my eyes closed, my heart open, her lips would have been just as soft as any other's, and her mouth as warm, tender and loving. You forget things like that, sometimes, don't look away enough. You see things, even when you're not looking.

Of course, I'm not in love with her (not as much as Monica, who I kind of miss now she's stopped fluttering) but I find her a warm thing, a place to lose fears in. I like her, perhaps even half-love her.

When we left the cinema we ran into some trouble with yobbos, which might have passed without too much incident, except Mary had to open her mouth on them. '*Why don't you fuck off?'* she shouted, and that was the point they pursued us. I'm not a good runner really, I tend to look around too much, but that time I ran like a whippet. I still didn't catch Mary up, she was two streets ahead of me, but she's probably had more experience of that with her hit-and-run tactics of prostitution. They didn't stop chasing us, though, that's what I couldn't get over. I thought they'd give up after a mile or so. But no, right through the centre of town we went, down Deansgate, around Piccadilly Circus. I had some small change in my pocket and that had to bounce out, and I nearly got caught when I stopped for it. Nobody helped us, though, nobody said, 'Look at those guys!' Perhaps we looked like running dogs to them.

She's pretty street-wise, Mary is, really. She led me through a Steak and Kebab restaurant where we had quite an audience to watch us, and out of the back door into an alleyway, and still the mad hooligans pursued us. Not through the restaurant, they ran round the side of the building; I don't know who was smarter, maybe they were? What really amazed me, when we started running again, was that she stuffed a bread roll in my pocket. 'Save that for later,' she said, 'I only got two of them.'

'Where'd you get them from?'

'The fat bloke with glasses.'

I've never been chased before, not since my childhood, and it's funny how you get to enjoy it. Only when you're winning, of course, when they're not actually gaining on you, but when you're winning it can be exhilarating. I started shouting back to them, giving encouragement to try to keep up with us, which is the point at which I ran into the lamppost. Fortunately, they'd just given up at that stage because I knocked myself totally senseless (and got a black eye) and Mary practically had to carry me home from there. I've never been hurt like that, sudden and blinding, my whole head felt like an eruption. I felt sick to the bottom of my stomach.

It didn't stop aching for at least three days after that. But at least we got away with the bread rolls, and there's something about physical injury which does you good. I mean, pain makes you forget everything else, and people fuss around you, making you into something special (it helps them too). You can't go mad or die from some awful creeping disease while you're lying about injured because there's some law of the universe which says you can only suffer one serious thing at a time. It helps you slow down, too. You're forced to lie on your back and think of things in a rational way. You're kind of outside the human race for a while. Hijackers often let sick hostages go, preferring to terrorise and torture the fit and well, even though they plan to shoot everyone in the end, even though they're already busy shooting people once an hour when their demands remain unheeded. The next victim is told to walk down the aisle to the exit door. He looks up at the terrorist with yellow eyes that don't give a damn. 'He *can't* walk to the plane steps. He's got malaria,' says the man's wife, cradling his head in her lap. They make concessions towards the sick without thinking how ludicrous they are. 'We'll let this one go. He looks really ill. I don't think he's faking it. Look at the colour of his skin.' They kill the man's wife though. She's got no excuse. She isn't sick like her husband.

Then, when you start to get better, the world looks more rosy than before, for some reason. There's a sort of relief in the air, as if you've been given a second chance. Those who have looked after you feel good too, because they've had a chance to prove how charitable they are. And because you've got well they feel successful. When the hijackers are finally captured, they are considered humane people because they let the ambulance take away the man with malaria.

Mary is kind of adventurous, really, and things happen around her. She'd lose you if you tried to keep up with her. She has no time to think of things, she's too busy doing them. I'm cautious, I'd not last five minutes. (I forgot to say she also vandalised the cinema seat. I don't know why she did that, just spite I guess.) And she's excellent at shoplifting, something at which I am totally inept. But she comes out with all sorts, with soup plates and alarm clocks, and I say to her, 'What do you want all this for?' 'I don't,' she says, and throws it away again. I think she simply does it as a pastime. Once she came out with a roll of electric flex and said, 'That'll come in really handy.' But she never did use it and it's still in the house somewhere, probably with our collection. I say, 'Steal some useful things,' and she says, 'You steal them.' And she has a point there, so I don't bother criticising.

The one thing against Mary, and it is quite a big thing, is that she's got one crazy boyfriend.

Mary's boyfriend doesn't like me because I spend so much time with his girlfriend. The fact that it's a platonic thing and if he cared for her he'd spend more time with her doesn't appear to enter into his thinking. I don't think a lot does. Some men are philosophers and some men are doers, and her man's a blot on the landscape.

I don't know what her boyfriend is, a van driver, lounge lizard, a man who collects glasses in old public houses, he's all of these things and probably others too. He might be a fighter, a bar tender, a drunkard, a man in a street brawl, but one thing he isn't is pretty. He must be so ugly it would weigh against him if he went for a permanent job. So he enjoys life in fragments: a few words in this place, a few hours at that firm, he scrapes things, he cobbles existence. I asked Mary why she likes him, she said, 'He makes me laugh.' He'd have to do something for her, he can't play on good looks he looks like a man-meets-potato. Yet at the same time he looks like the kind of man who has no difficulty attracting women to him. It's all down to confidence, breaking the ground rules; it's hard for him, yet it's so easy.

I've never seen a man who looks at me with quite such vehement hatred. He abhors every pore of me, loathes all my follicles, he hates me as Jews hated Jesus. This is purely a chemical thing, I've done nothing to him; he loathes me because I'm existing. There will come a day, I half expect, when he drives a blade between my shoulders. The only thing saving me is that Mary's around me. If she leaves me, he'll come looking for me. And rather than frightening, or attempting to intimidate him, I try to get into his good books. I almost fawn around him, and he practically vomits at this, and I wish I could stop it, but he scares me. His foul breath disgusts me, his lank hair distresses me, but I try so damn hard to be liked by him. Of all the people in all the world it's the one I hate most who I fawn to. I must have no backbone, I must have no principles, but, for God's sake, this man strikes such fear in me.

I don't know where he lives but, if I did, I'd go and burn it down. I seldom stop thinking about him, though I just as seldom have to see him, for he's not an attentive kind of boyfriend. He leaves her alone for ten days at a time, and then he comes in like he owns the place. He struts like a gigolo, preens like a peacock, he's filthy, the smell thunders from him.

He brings his mad sidekicks round, warpaint and greaseballs. We all have a party (but I don't). I've long been a wall-flower, since I was a youngster. Their revels do nothing to unwind me. If there was a table I would be hiding under it, but I try to sit bravely and smile at them, laugh at their wisecracks. This takes a great effort from me and I end up with a migraine, but they'd like that, I guess, they'd heap scorn on it. (It's a point worth discussing, whether threatening people ever find themselves suffering from migraines. Maybe it's a more 'sensitive' affliction.)

Marty, the boyfriend, has got some scheme planned for me. He wants me to participate in something. Even before I knew what it was I guessed it was something criminal.

What it is, is this: he wants to use my bedroom for stashing some stuff he's stolen. I feel rather fond of my bedroom, and I don't like to abuse it this way, but if he wants it I'm not going to argue with him. I hope it's not heroin. He's so low-level, it will probably turn out to be hot teddy bears nicked from a fairground.

On that comforting thought I retire to my bedroom, and wonder what the morning will bring me.

But the party still goes on, it rings through my darkness. There's no real escape from anything. Sometimes I think to myself, I'll go out and find someone, a woman, just to do it with. No strings. Just to get rid of the tension, to escape for a few seconds into that other world. But you can't do that, just find someone feeling exactly like you feel at that moment, someone willing to have sex for the sake of it. Oh there are plenty of them out there, but they're atoms, swirling in the cosmos. I could go and look for a prostitute I suppose, but I've always felt intimated by them. I don't think they like men very much at all (why should they?) and they say things they *think* all men want to hear.

'Hello, big boy. You look a strong guy. Want to come in and show me your muscles?'

The first prostitute who leans out of the window of her flat wearing glasses and hair done up in a wispy bun, calling out, 'Hey, you look a nice man. I think you have a sensitive face. Why don't you come on in and talk for a while?' is going to make an absolute fortune.

DOG PEOPLE: SEVENTEEN

This morning I was in one of the precincts in the centre of town when I saw a sign on a door.

SOCIAL SERVICES: AREA OFFICE

I pushed open the door and walked in. The place was like a zoo, an open zoo, with animals rushing around all over the place and phones ringing which no one seemed to be taking any notice of. There were mostly women, but some men. I stood for a long time by a phone that simply rang and rang on an empty desk. The caller must have had the patience of a trilobite waiting to evolve. Either that or they knew that once you had a line into this place you hung onto it until the Second Coming, because you wouldn't get another one. Finally, a pudgy young woman with dark hair picked it up while passing the desk.

'Hello? No, he's not in at the moment, sorry. What? Oh, the hospital. Some client of his bit him and he's gone to get a blood test. No, sorry, can't help you. Got my own case load to deal with and anyway he's got his reports with him. Try tomorrow.'

She put the phone down and saw me staring.

'Is anyone dealing with you?' she asked. 'Who did you come to see?'

She didn't seem to mind that I was covered in dirt, probably had fleas and that my clothes were filthy rags. At least she didn't say so and neither did her eyes. She looked about seventeen.

'Are you a social worker?' I asked.

'Yes. Who was it you wanted to see? Are you one of John Baker's clients? He's not in today.'

'I know,' I said. 'He got bitten by a rabid client.'

She frowned. 'No he didn't. John's in court today. Look, what do you want? I'm pretty busy...'

'Busy, what? Taking people's babies? Or leaving them there to get bashed?'

She sighed, deeply, her pudgy face quivering.

'Popular image. The gutter press don't do us any favours, do they? Two seconds. What do you want?'

'Money,' I replied promptly.

'Wrong place. You need Social Security. We don't have money here. I can give you a note to take round to them, if you like. I suppose you want lodgings and a meal?'

Someone called to her and she looked at the watch on her chubby wrist.

'God, twelve-thirty already?'

'Buy me a cup of coffee,' I said. 'I need to talk to someone.'

She looked irritated.

'Please Susan? It's your lunch hour. I'm not as dirty as I look.'

'How did you...oh,' she realised that I had got the name from the man who had called to her. 'Look, this is my own time.'

I shrugged. 'I'm just asking. Is there a canteen here? You'll be safe. Bring Tarzan along with you.' I indicated to the man who was busy tidying papers on his desk.

'That won't be necessary,' she said, tight-lipped. 'I've snatched babies out of psychopaths' arms, so I'm hardly likely to be frightened of you, am I?'

'You look about seventeen.'

'I'm twenty-three - and you look fifty, though I guess you're probably in your thirties. Come on then - and don't get too close. I've smelled sweeter sewers.'

At least she was direct. I like blunt people. They're easier to talk to. She took a coat off a peg by the door and I followed her out. No one seemed to think it was unusual, a tramp going through the doorway with a pristine-clean twenty-three year old girl, as if they were going out on the town.

We didn't go to a canteen. We went to a place called Hoagy's, in a backstreet. I didn't care where we went as long as I got my cup of coffee. My throat was as dry as the Sahara, and I had a thick lip where Mary had kicked me. Her boyfriend had come in drunk, taken a swing at me at last. I ducked, fell over. Mary went to kick her boyfriend on the shin and caught me in the mouth instead. I scrambled to my feet and left the house, leaving her and the van driver to battle it out.

'Two cups of coffee,' said Susan to the waitress, 'and - do you want anything to eat?'

'Egg and chips,' I mumbled.

'- egg and chips, and some bread I suppose. Thank you.'

The waitress left us.

'Thanks a lot,' I said.

She sighed. 'Don't mention it. Half my meagre earnings go on egg and chips for lost people. Just don't give me fleas that's all.'

'Eh?'

'The last one gave me fleas. They were hopping all over her collar.' She shuddered.

'I haven't *got* fleas,' I said indignantly. 'At least, I don't think so. I don't itch,' I scratched, 'or didn't until you mentioned them. I'm just a little cracked at the moment, that's all. My wife died.'

She looked sympathetic.

'Oh, I'm sorry.'

'That's okay. It was over a year ago - but I think I'm getting post-trauma-something. What do you call it?'

'I don't know. I'm not a psychiatric social worker, though I did work for the General Hospital for a while.'

'They have special social workers for nut cases?'

She smiled. 'Listen, let me educate you a little into the ways of social services. Despite what you read in the papers, we don't work only with abused children. We help with the mentally ill, the infirm, hospital after-care, the elderly, and a dozen other different areas. We get paid less than the lowest paid school teacher and sometimes have so many cases at one time that it's impossible to see them all more than once in six weeks - physically and timewise impossible - yet we're expected to help protect them. When we are worried about a child for instance, it takes a doctor's say so and a court order, which means convincing a magistrate that the child's in danger, before we can even begin to help. When something goes wrong - when we make a mistake and take a child away from innocent parents, or leave one there too long and it's injured - the press conveniently forget the doctor and the magistrate and promptly crucify the social worker. That's what we're there for. We're society's scapegoats.'

'Are you bitter?'

Her eyes went wide.

'No, as I said, that's what we're there for. The only people who get up my nose are the fat cat businessmen on the morning trains who humph about wasted public money on social workers. That maimed or dead child is *their* responsibility as much as anyone's, and they should damn well realise that if they want a system that works they have to pay for it. This is a dirty job with very little money around to make it work properly. The government seems to think that industry needs money to make it work, but social services can run on next to nothing. Everyone screams about 'the rights of the individual' and then expects us to know exactly what's going on inside our clients' homes. 'The poor parents,' they say, when we take a child away and it turns out to be a mistake - and mistakes are *always* going to happen because that's in the nature of the job - but it's the *child* who is our responsibility, not the parents.'

'I thought it was me who asked to talk to *you*,' I said.

She smiled again.

'You're right. I'm sorry. I just get so furious. Not *bitter*, just angry at the pathetic brainwashed readers of the gutter press. People of received opinions, too lazy to think things out for themselves. They scream blue murder when they find out that the social worker behind the 'scandal' isn't qualified, but they don't yell when the government refuses to increase the social services budget. How do they think people become qualified? It takes *money* - which they're not prepared to pay.'

I felt hot all over.

'They make ME sick!' I shouted, sharing her anger.

Several people in the café looked round at us, and Susan went red, probably thinking she had gone a bit too far.

'Eat your egg and chips,' she said quietly.

I did as she told me. She might have been a podgy twenty-three-year old (with a Derbyshire accent?) but she had an air of authority about her which couldn't be ignored.

'Okay,' she said, as I wiped round my plate with my bread, 'what's your story? Drink? You seem an intelligent man. You're not generally inadequate, are you?'

'No, I told you. I cracked up for a while. I'm feeling a bit better now. Things are a little more lucid lately.'

She leaned forward, her chin on her hands. There was a little gold signet ring on the middle finger of her left hand, which cut into her chubbiness. I wondered if she had ever had a boyfriend, outside of school that is. Probably not.

'You ought to see someone,' she said. 'A doctor.'

'I told you - I'm getting better. Just takes time, that's all.'

'These things go in cycles. I know that much. You'll probably have a relapse soon, and it will be worse. Maybe not, but you ought to see someone anyway.'

'Aren't you supposed to humour me? Tell me I'm fine, looking great? And then sneak out to phone the funny farm?'

'The worse thing anyone can do is lie to someone who's mentally ill - not that you *are* - I can't tell you. When they're in a clear period they remember that they've been lied to, and then all the trust is gone. I told you, I worked in a hospital. If you told me you could see little green men I would tell you that I couldn't...'

'Unless there really *were* little green men in the room.'

'Steven Spielberg notwithstanding,' she laughed.

'Can I sleep with you Susan?' I asked.

She flushed just a little, then her complexion cleared. She seemed amused.

'You're trying to shock me.'

'No I'm not. I really want to sleep with you.'

'Well you can't, because I don't want to, and anyway I'm married - happily married.'

I was aghast. 'You're only twenty-three - and you don't wear a ring. Not a wedding ring.'

'That's my choice, nevertheless I'm married. I married at eighteen and before you say anything, *two*-thirds of them work.'

'What do you mean?'

'Everyone keeps saying, 'A third of marriages end in divorce these days.' No one ever says, 'Two thirds of the marriages work all the way to the grave.' Anyway, I don't fancy you, certainly not in your present condition, and I don't think you fancy me, really. I think you're trying to work something out of your head, and you think something like that would do it. It won't. See a doctor.'

'You're pretty blunt for a young girl,' I said, angry.

'Maybe. I don't think the bedside manner - wrong phrase under the circumstances. I don't think being nice helps in situations like this.'

'Are you sure you couldn't like me?' I wheedled. 'If I cleaned myself up. I'm really not bad looking...'

'It's got nothing to do with that,' she snapped. 'I love someone and I'm certainly not going to put that in jeopardy just for an afternoon's experience. You wouldn't like it either. You're not the type. Listen, you won't find your wife - what was her name?'

'Angela.' I almost choked on the word.

'You won't find Angela again in anyone else. Especially not in a one afternoon stand. If she's dead, as you say she is, then she's gone. There'll be someone else, but it won't be her you know.'

'I know. It's Monica.'

'Then why don't you go to Monica. Have you got her telephone number?'

'Yes.'

'If you give it to me, I'll call her for you.'

'She probably hates me now.'

'She's probably worried sick about you.'

I suppose that was true, but I wasn't ready for Monica yet. Perhaps I never would be. I wanted to get back to the house, to see Mary. Who were all these women in my life? Mary, Monica, Susan - no Susan was *not* in my life. Neither was Mary, really. Who did I think I was, some kind of Don Juan? Even Monica would probably do without me very well, as the song goes.

I stood up, because I grew tired of just sitting there.

'Thanks for the talk...and the meal. I'll pay you back sometime.'

'Sure. Look, I'd like you to let me call Monica.'

I shook my head.

'Sorry, rights of the individual and all that. I want to stay nutty for a while longer. When I'm ready - ' Maybe I would never be ready. I still had to work this thing out with my fellow squatters. I had to be one of the dog people for a while. The dog people didn't have to do anything or be anyone. They took their personalities from others, lived only in the situation at hand, were just *there.* It was good to have no responsibilities. I knew now how the dog people from my own house had felt. They didn't even have to talk to me. They were just *there* and nothing else. I was an amoeba, floating around in the liquid of life, splitting off into a different personality every now and then. I had everything inside me still. I had violence in there, waiting to blast its way out. If I got *really* sick I might be one of those that killed half a dozen people before blowing my brains out. I didn't think I was - I hate hurting anyone, anything - but I was afraid I might be. God, I was so *scared* most of the time, and of what? I didn't damn well know. I was scared of nothing and everything. Just flaming scared, inside-out scared. People, places, situations, everything had me quaking in terror. There were those times when I said to myself, 'Pull it together, moron. You're a *man* for Christ's sake. What's Angela thinking of you now? What if Monica could see you, frightened to go outdoors, frightened to stay indoors? What are you, a wimp?' and for a moment I would feel like my old self. The courage would come back, flashflooding through me. But it would wash right over the top and disappear like a wave over the horizon. And I would cry:

'YES. YES I'M SCARED OF MY OWN SHADOW I'M TERRIFIED. ARE YOU SATISFIED?'

And I might be out on the street when I did this, and people would turn and look, and hurry on, or cluck their tongues. Mostly they would hurry on, because I was a nut and you can catch the fear from nuts like it's a virus. It can work on your sleep, until maybe you're the one lying awake, in terror of all things.

I went home, to the squat, and everyone was out except Mary. She was asleep on the stairs, so I left her there. I went into the kitchen and found seven bags of moth balls on the window sill. Mary had been shopping again, in her lightfingered way. Hell, what good were mothballs? I popped one in my mouth but it tasted foul, so I spat it out. We didn't even have any moths that I knew of. Why couldn't she have stolen Mars bars or something? There seemed to be some law at work in Mary which said she couldn't steal anything useful. It had to be something we couldn't eat or sell to the junk shop. Once, she took a dozen newly-baked bread rolls, but gave them away to some kids before she got back to the house. We were all starving but she gave them to some children who had probably had three breakfasts and a bag full of sweets by nine o'clock in the morning. You couldn't control Mary. She was bent on making a difficult life that much harder for us all. (If we said anything she just told us to go out and nick our own stuff. We were all too scared). Mary had been caught several times, but she always seemed to get away with it, either by pleading with the shopkeeper, or by getting violent and running. Once, she bit a store detective's hand. (I remembered Susan's phone call. Maybe Mary had been the 'client'.) Mary was fond of biting people. I wish she'd bitten the head off her boyfriend's shoulders, but she never did anything you wanted her to. She just pinched mothballs and greetings cards and hose pipe clips and rubber washers and bicycle pump valves and wax fruit and address books and grommets (? that's what it said on the bag - little brass eyelets) and paper napkins and a ballcock and three cans of stain remover and a whole aluminium girder, six feet long and bow ties and a drum of tar which she rolled all the way from a building site and a box of Pond's cold cream and a bottle of *Paco Rabanne* aftershave (which we drank) and a trombone slide (which she removed from the instrument while hiding behind a piano because she couldn't get the whole thing down her trouser leg) and black handkerchiefs and Tupperware container lids and six packets of Saxa salt and fancy coat hanger covers and toothbrush holders and seventy-eight bookmarks and on and on and on -

I fell asleep. It was the middle of the afternoon but I fell asleep on my bed in the squat. Like a dog I could fall asleep any time. I may have dreamed, I can't remember, but then I don't remember many things these days, a man of many personalities has trouble remembering things. My name is Steven Roberts and I'm thirty-seven years old and failing, at least I remember that much of myself. And I once had a wife name of Angela. I wanted to crack up (I still remember that much) but I didn't know how to go about it. So I tried to invent it, and went through the motions but, really, I still don't believe it. You cannot crack up when you think so hard on it, the insane never think that they're insane.

So what was I doing? I was stalling for time somehow, knowing that one day I would go back. There might not be much to go back to but at least there would be a direction to work in and it couldn't be much worse than it had been previously. I had a lot of things that I didn't want: a job that I didn't enjoy and a house that I'd grown tired of living in - at least I could get those things out of my system. A dog only lives for the moment.

Maybe I was thinking these things when I woke up, I don't know, it was kind of confusing. There were muffled bangings in the building and lights flashing and somebody talking to me, and I had the feeling that somebody was crawling onto my bed.

'What's happening?' I said.

'It's only me,' said Mary. 'There's someone to see you.'

'Who?' I said, sitting up, switching on a bicycle lamp.

'A woman. I don't know. She says her name's Susan.'

'Susan? What's she doing here? What time is it anyway?'

'Nine o'clock.'

'I hope I'm not disturbing you.' This time it was Susan's voice, and she appeared through the gap in the wall behind Mary, and the two women sat on my mattress.

I didn't say anything. I was too weary. I looked at them and just sat there groaning.

'Well,' said Mary after a moment, 'I'll leave you to get on with your business. Call if you want anything - champagne or oysters. We've got lots of things in the larder.'

'Ha, ha,' I murmured. 'Send us some moth balls. We're doing a great deal on moth balls.'

Mary left us and I looked at Susan and ruffled my hands through my hairstyle. 'Wasn't expecting a visitor,' I told her. 'Though there's not much I could do if I had been.'

Susan looked around the room, which was dark and drab and dusty, in many ways more like a cellar than a bedroom. 'This is how you live?' she said.

I nodded. 'It's not much of anything. It's all kind of stupid, really. Lots of things going for me, this is the way I end up. My wife would be rather ashamed of me.'

'Not necessarily,' she murmured, adjusting her position on the mattress. 'But I was rather concerned about you myself, I came to see if you'd like to go for a drink.'

'A drink?' I said. 'I'm not really dressed for it. I'm not really dressed up for anything.'

'That doesn't matter. The main thing's that we sit and have a talk about things. You've got to get yourself on the tracks again.'

'I know that.' I nodded. 'I've known that a long time, ever since I walked out on my own home.'

'So let's go and talk about, see if we can't fix it,' she said. 'The best thing for loneliness is company.'

'Are you lonely, too?' I asked her.

'Not in the same way. But everyone's lonely in some way.'

It seemed like a good thing to do so I got up and pulled on the best of my clothing and had such a wash as I could get in the sink downstairs and went out and let Susan lead me. We didn't go far, to the first pub we came to, to a seat in the corner, to talking. She put a glass in front of me and said, 'Is this how you want it to be now?'

'How?' I said. 'What do you mean?'

'Spending your life in a hovel.'

'Oh no,' I said, letting my eyes wander idly. 'It's only a temporary setback.'

'You want to talk about it?'

I looked at her. 'Is this where you use your psychology?'

'Something like that.' She smiled.

I shrugged. 'I'll talk about it. I suppose. I'm a good talker.' I took one of her cigarettes and rolled it around in an ashtray. I tried to find a place I could start things. 'This is a bit late for you,' I said, finding something else to distract me a moment. 'Shouldn't you be home now? Doesn't your husband get to miss you?'

'I'm not married,' she said. 'I only say that because it's easier than getting into difficulties.'

'Oh,' I said, nodding. 'Is this because I'm worthy? Are you trying to get me back to normality?'

'I don't think you ought to just waste yourself.'

'You're right,' I said. I took her hand and held it for a minute and said, 'For what it's worth, I do appreciate it. Even though I might appear, sometimes, cynical.'

'I know,' she said. 'Everyone likes attention.'

I laughed, she was smarter than I was. I let go of her hand and said, 'They're very warm, you've got nice hands. I think you're a nice person overall.'

'So why don't you tell me how your wife died?'

And that made me go silent for a while. It was something I thought about, thought about a great deal, but didn't often actually talk about. It's the kind of thing that people don't really want to hear, it's one of those things that are too personal. They don't mind the death, it's the dying they're wary of. Most people don't want to hear about it.

Nor do I often have the will power to talk about it. 'She drove into a tree,' I said, 'and had massive abdominal and chest injuries. She must have died almost immediately. My son, who was with her, was sent through the windscreen, but left most of his legs on the dashboard. He wasn't strapped in at all. Not that it would have made a great deal of difference, the bonnet ended up on the back seat.'

'He died too?' said Susan.

'Oh yes, he was definitely dead. Him you could not even recognise, though I had to go down and try to pretend so. I had to look at both of them, to confirm that it really was my family. But it wasn't my family, though I couldn't really tell them that. It was two heaps of meat, on two trolleys.'

'Please don't cry,' she said.

'I can't really help crying. And, anyway, I want to,' I snivelled.

She gave me a handkerchief to cry into.

'Then I went home,' I said, 'and sat for a long time and kept being sick while I thought about them. I guess, when you think about it, if you ever get to think about it, that you hope that your family will die easily, they'll maybe die in their sleep without knowing. You don't think they're going to die smashed up and broken, looking like things you might find in a slaughterhouse. It was very upsetting. I mean, the whole thing was upsetting, but, seeing them like that was upsetting. I guess that I hadn't been the most perfect husband, and she'd probably not been all that good either. But you do all you can for each other, even when it's not going right. The last thing you need is to lose them. I'd even thought that I wanted other women sometimes - I wonder if all of us do? - and afterwards, when I was free to do as I pleased, I didn't really want anyone but my family back. Do you think God plays with our feelings? Makes us want things when we can't have them, then not want them when we can? I felt guilty too, about that. Through all the years I suppose I was happy. I didn't want her dying like a rag doll.

'I tried to bury them.' I'd finally stopped crying, but I was staring hard at the table and I forced myself away from it, because I needed to. 'You know, you dig a pit inside your heart and try to lose them in it. But it doesn't really work that way, you have to face them one day. You have to face the new situation, not just cling on to the memory. I tried to hide them for that first year, and all that I did was delay things. Sooner or later they had to come out again, and that's what they did on the anniversary. Everything seemed to become rather pointless. They gave me the chance to go crazy.'

'Is that what you've been doing? Making yourself crazy?'

'I guess so. I think I'm sincere about it.'

A few minutes passed while we sat quietly drinking and I thought just how far away it seemed at that moment: it was over a full year since they died now. Perhaps it was time to get over the loss, maybe I'd been using it as an excuse. You never stop hurting but, really, you're over it, you just act out the motions of grieving. Maybe. Maybe, I wanted to be over it, to stop wasting my time on this sadness. Too much time wasted - perhaps it's not Angela but the fact of my own dull existence. I should have done something to make life important. Had they died so that I could just waste my own life?

Perhaps, at that moment, I started to come out of it. If there's a God, maybe He sent me Susan.

I don't think she realised this, she was just trying to help me, but at the end of the day you make your own luck. I picked out Susan and she then responded to me. She gave me hope when I needed it.

I picked up her hand again and gave her my brave smile. 'You're a very useful person to have around,' I said.

'Why's that?' she said.

'You're good at your job. You didn't mean to, but you've given me some purpose.'

She smiled, a slightly awkward smile. 'All I did was take you out for a drink.'

'It's the small things that matter, they make all the difference.'

'Then I wish I'd bought a drink for you a long time ago.' She looked around. I don't suppose she knew what I was talking about, but I did, and that's all that mattered.

'I've been drifting for a long time,' I said. 'I thought nobody wanted me. I was wrong, everybody is needed. I went into a kind of blackness, but there's no such thing as total darkness, there's always a thread of light somewhere. I don't know how to explain this to you but just by attending to me you've given me more hope than I've seen in the offing for a long time. I went into your office because I was full of self-pity. You did the very best thing that you could for me.'

'What was that?'

'You took me for coffee. I asked for it, and you actually gave it to me.'

She smiled again. 'You're very simple.'

'I know. And I thought I was so complicated.'

'I don't understand you,' she said.

'I don't know that I do. But I'm desperately glad that you called for me.'

She took me home with her, I don't know why, there was never any suggestion of togetherness. Perhaps she was lonely, perhaps she was scared for me, perhaps, like a child, I just begged for it. Whatever it was we must have both had a need of it, it was something that neither of us questioned.

I had a bath while she washed my clothes through then we sat by her fire while she dried them. She lived in a small flat with precious little space in it and we seemed to be surrounded by bookcases. They towered all around us, they groaned through their burdens; I have never seen so many books before.

'Do you read all these books?' I said.

'Some of them. I collect them, though. I collect them, even though I won't read them.'

'That's what our life is like, things we might read one day. I like that, we need to have something.' That's what my life lacked, I failed to find something to replace the family which left me. I should have let Monica in, I should have found something, but all that I did was to lose things. I made a mistake there. Even people like Mary, even they have a purpose, even though I can't really discern it. But she keeps on hoping, and she keeps on stealing – and suddenly I knew why she steals useless items, it's so she never is forced to depend on it. The stealing's a game for life, something beside it; if she stole for life, life would be over. I knew that, and smiled then. All these people had helped me; people, normally, I'd not come into contact with, because I wasted my life on the Franklyns and Barnetts, and really there are so many more there.

'I'm kind of glad I ran away,' I said. 'It will make it much easier to go back again.'

'Will you go back?' she said.

'Not at this moment though. At this moment I just need to talk about it.' And also at that moment I knew that I wanted, and was about to have a relationship with Susan. A moment we both knew, which is why we were sitting there. A moment we desperately needed.

It was something I hadn't done for a very long time now, it was something I thought I'd forgotten. But I hadn't forgotten, it was just lying dormant. We all have a great love inside us.

I moved my remaining things out of the squat and said goodbye to Mary. In a way that was kind of an emotional moment because she also felt what I was feeling. We have love inside us, it just needs that moment in which it can find its expression. We clung on to each other so that we might never lose it, we squeezed it inside us like heartbeats; and just for a moment we branded ourselves with it, and burned ourselves inside that feeling.

'You'd better take care of yourself,' she cried.

'You too. Keep on stealing!' And we laughed, like we'd found something wonderful. 'You'd better not lose it!'

'Nor you,' she said, knowing it all. 'And one day I'll find you to check on it!'

I gave her my address down south and she gave me an address I could contact her at, though we both knew we might never use them. But that's not important, it's the fact of that knowing. It's the fact that there's someone there caring for us.

It's the fact that that darkness is still full of starlight. It's the fact that we're greater than animals.

DOG PEOPLE: NINETEEN

What is a love affair? God knows, I am only human, He didn't give me words to describe it. Poets and philosophers far more spiritual, far more intellectual than me, have been trying to work it out since Adam met Eve. It's something that will provide substance for writers and thinkers until the end of time, because there seems to be no definition, no answers. There are only affirmations or denials, or modifications and alterations. ('I *am* in love with him.' 'I am *not* in love with her.' 'I *thought* I was in love with you, but it was something else.') In truth, no one knows what love is, nor will they ever. What it remains is an attraction, sometimes strong, sometimes weak, sometimes fatal. A single or dual magnetism. A fulfilled or unfulfilled set of needs.

Since no one knows what love is, it follows that they do not know what is a love affair.

To me, an affair is a thing of fear and terror, of lust and of longing and of stomach ache (for I ache in my guts when I'm longing). And the best thing of all is that this love affair was a temporary thing from the start, and knowing its briefness we took all we could from it, and we shed all that fear we might shrink from. And, for that time, I loved her like madness.

It lasted for twenty-eight days, it was love encapsulated: something to put in a small bottle, a vial, and treasure like a pressed flower. We didn't have time to make the normal awful mistakes, to lie to each other, destroy one another's faith. Nothing was taken for granted, nothing rushed, no stages missed, we acted as if it was holy (which is surely how all love should be). There was no clumsy clambering between warm bed-sheets, no fumbling, no grappling, no panting nor lunging; we made no false promises, called for no favours and knew that it would not last long because we kept asking things like, 'How long do you think it will last?' There is no need of such questions when you're engaged in a true love, for true love assumes it's forever. But that did not diminish it, nor were its pleasures the less sweet. Indeed perhaps they were intensified. It's a long time since I've been so loved.

How did it start? It started almost immediately. It started from the moment I moved my belongings, and plunged into fearsome attraction. It has been a long time since I courted, I forgot how much nervousness lies there. It's adolescent, its fears never lessen, nor do our years make them alter. And it could have been so very different, we could have gone to bed that first night. But we didn't. A strange kind of shyness came over the both of us. Two lonely people made nervous. I was fearful of not impressing her. I wanted her to like everything about me, everything I'd done. A minor criticism would have torn the heart from me. I said things I would never normally say to anyone, in a kind of half-dream state, as if I was twelve years of age. That first stage of love - infatuation - call it what you like - it never really grows up. It stays the same age inside all of us. We grow to adulthood, but that first flush of love remains as old as when it was born, usually about twelve years after us.

'Where should I sleep?' I said, when we returned to her flat, clutching my clothing in armfuls.

'Erm - I don't know,' she said, looking around her. 'Where would you like to?'

'On the sofa?'

She smiled then. 'I think that the sofa will be fine for you.'

'Me too.' We dragged it into a better position.

Strange how readily we talked in the early day, yet now we were tongue-tied and nervous. 'I'll put my toothbrush in the bathroom.'

'Just use the place like your own.'

I couldn't do that, it was quite clearly her place, full of her feminine objects. And feminine objects are cute and alarming, their hairbrushes, trinkets and photographs. 'Who are these pictures?' I said, picking a frame up.

'They're my family. That's my mother, my sister, my brother.'

'Where's your dad?'

'He died some years ago.'

'Oh. I'm sorry.'

'And this is the dog.'

We spent a long time studying the dog's picture, it was a fine German Shepherd with eyes of hot amber; it stared right at the lens of the camera. 'I've never had a dog,' I said. 'I had some people who acted like dogs, and I had a small goat for a while. But never a real dog, not like your Sasha. I think that I'm rather afraid of them.'

'You shouldn't be afraid,' she said, 'it's the only thing which really unnerves them. If you treat them like people and just move around them, they're happy to take you for granted.'

'I'll try to remember that.'

'But never forget,' she said. 'At the end of the day, they're just animals.'

'Right. I will try to remember.'

Her hand touched mine when she retrieved the picture and the spot burned as if I had been touched by a red hot poker. I think she knew because she looked at me in a kind of startled way, almost dropping the photo.

'I'll just put on some tea,' she said in a squeaky voice.

'Okay,' I replied, my own voice lost somewhere down at the bottom of my throat.

When she brought the tea back into the room, she sat next to me on the sofa and I could feel the warmth of her chubby thigh through the cotton dress she wore. My muscles went rigid and I was afraid to move in case I lost that warm patch of thigh, or she suddenly realised I was stealing her electricity and pulled away from me. (She told me later that she was just as nervous, just as vibrant.) We looked through a magazine together, not reading the words, brushing arms (those soft hairs full of static!) and feeling the heat of one another's cheek. The pictures in the magazine began to blur and then I felt her arm around my shoulder. She had done something, quite naturally, that youths sweat over for hours and get into all sorts of contorted positions in order to do it without seeming obvious about it. I remember sitting in a cinema, or on such a sofa, my arm draped across the back of the seat in an advanced state of pins and needles, thinking, 'My limb's going dead. There's no blood in it. The damn seat's cut off my circulation. Dare I? *Dare* I?' And in the end, my arm flopping back to my side, fearful of the distorted face of rejection: '*What* are you *doing*?' Later, when I had mastered the art of arm-shouldering, having the same dilemma over whether to touch a breast or not.

Susan took care of that too, lifting my limp hand while we were kissing, and placing it carefully over one of her breasts. Inside, my head exploded with gratitude and warmth. I think I might have killed for her at that moment. I would certainly have died for her.

God knows why she took me in, God knows why she liked me. God knows what she hoped to gain from me, maybe for nothing but company. Whatever it was, I was glad of the chance of it, I put the best of my life down to Susan. She gave me affection and gave me attention when I was really approaching my lowest. Women are god-like, I've always admired that. Susan showed me why they deserve it.

'I'm not very lucky,' she said, 'in my relationships, and I'm not the most attractive one around. I ought to be dieting, and trying to look stylish, but really you need somebody there for it.'

'Do it for me,' I said. 'Work for each other.'

We did, and we shed so much torpor.

Twenty-eight days of getting to know someone, twenty-eight days of exploring. So little time but such precious moments, I lived, like I'd almost forgotten.

She is not the most physically attractive woman I have known, but some people say beauty is not on the outside, and it wasn't until Susan I believed that. Beauty is gentleness and taking the time for someone, and listening to their problems without baulking. Did we have many problems? Oh yes, we were cursed with them; I had a whole year to explain to myself. What was I doing, going crazy, undermining things? Because there was nobody there I could talk to. I should have talked to Monica but we were too busy explaining things. *This is what's wrong and this is how to make sense of things.* And all the time we were just losing them. I made a mistake trying to shift burdens onto her, and really she wasn't that strong for them. Some people aren't there to make life work out for you, some people are just there for living. I should have loved Monica, but I let her start to irritate me; I thought that the lifestyle was *Monica.*

'Do you know what I mean?' I said, talking to Susan.

'I think so. They can't all understand us.'

'No, you're right. We think that we know them and they should understand us, but, really, that's not what they're there for. Good God, I can't even begin to understand my own self. And how little effort did I give to her?'

'Hush,' she said, and brushed some hair from my brow. I looked at her. She was so thoughtful.

'Why are you thoughtful, and why are you alone?' I said.

'Because some people have to wait longer.'

'You're very philosophical.'

'No, I'm not really. I'm just very patient,' she murmured.

There was so much I could learn from her.

'Do you think you can stop being patient now?'

Her face grew a little serious.

'We're not made for each other in that way, Steven. I don't want to hurt you, but I think you know that. We're two people passing each other in a desert - you've only got water and I've only got food, and we're sharing them. But once we're a bit stronger we'll go on from there, probably different ways.'

I felt very sad. I could have choked out words I didn't mean, just to make us both think she was wrong, but I knew she wasn't. It was kind of beautiful in a way, the temporary nature of it all, but sad just the same. Her little speech had been rehearsed. No one can think of things like that to say spontaneously. But it was still genuine. I felt it.

'You're very young,' I said.

She snuggled up to me.

'I know. I have plenty of time.'

'And mine's running out?' I said.

'No, you have time too, it's just that you have less than me. You've had some of yours. I've not been married, nor had a child, nor even a permanent lover really. You've had all of those things. I know you lost them, very savagely, but you would have done anyway, in the end, slowly. Your child would have grown and your wife, well, something else might have happened. You might have fallen in love with Monica, or Angela with someone else. You might have grown away from one another. Who knows? Whatever, you had it, and nothing's permanent is it? I want some of those things, but not now. Not yet.'

'You're very young,' I said. But not as young as your thirty-seven-year old companion.

DOG PEOPLE: TWENTY

Thus I came back to the man I had once been, and I knew it was time to go home again. I'd known for a long time I'm not a man on the outskirts, I am a man who belongs in his own life. It might not be much of a life, but it's the life that I've made for myself, and I guess it's my duty to live through it. Squatting in Manchester, good as it seems at times, is not really meant for people like me, it's for people like Mary, to whom it comes naturally. Or if they're not born to it at least they make sense of it. My kind don't know what to do with it. In a way we rather waste it because we still want our comforts. I really like sleeping in warm beds. It took me a while to arrive at this conclusion, and I went a little crazy on the way there. But at least I learned something, there are no easy roads through life, and if there were we'd have already found them.

So I finally moved my few things from Susan's house and she helped me load them into the Sigma. On the steps of her condo we said our goodbyes to each other because, like squatting, our affair had no future. She and I both realised that, though it didn't stop a rush of tears, but at least we broke up like two lovers. That's the best way for it, to leave bridges open, knowing we may never use them. Perhaps she's the best friend I ever encountered in life. Perhaps she's the life I was looking for.

Anyway I returned to the squat to say goodbye to Mary, only to discover that she'd already moved on somewhere, and somebody said that she has her own flat (someone else said that she's also on probation!) So it's nice to know that some things are constant. But she must have suspected that I would be coming back because she left a brief note in the hallway for me. It didn't say much, it just said - *You take care of yourself. And don't take up stealing, you're no good!* She had also ditched her crazy boyfriend which I considered, overall, was a wise move. But I hope she keeps stealing, and I hope she gets away with it. And I hope that she'll come see me some day.

And after that there was nothing to hold me to Manchester, and no reason to keep me from homecoming. But I drive around the city once or twice, just to check the life I left behind, and I said a farewell to the Dog People. That was my last act, no more ties to hold me there. I turned the car south for the motorway.

I left in the evening, with the city bright behind me, and turned to the low, dying sunset.

I took the day easy, I was in no great hurry, and I wanted to savour the journey I was making. I'd brought a lot of memories with me and I hoped they'd be enough to sustain me, all bitter-sweet, all dark and all hopeful. And though you never know what the next day will present to you; I hoped I was strong enough to cope with it.

So in this frame of mind, and content with my brief rush into the nether world of squatters, I retraced my two hundred mile journey.

It was a false thing. There is no triumph in a warrior's homecoming when the war has not been a noble one. There is only a gradually growing sense of waste. As familiar sights came into view the old triggers began clicking, wheels and levers moved into motion. Over and over came the refrain, 'everything changes except the main problem, which will always remain'. I thought I had been away to war and had come home victorious, only to find that I'd been running away from the battle, and now I was coming back to find the fight still raging.

On the A127 I got the first taste of danger, the first hint of darkness inside me. This was the road on which my wife had to kill herself. And some fourteen months later, I was travelling the same highway.

I don't know why my spirits weakened, unless her sad ghost was haunting me. Perhaps I deluded myself, and I wasn't so healthy; perhaps I was at my most vulnerable. I once had a friend who said that suicides don't happen when a person is at their most hopeless. A suicide is most likely when you start to emerge again, when you climb out of deepest depression, for then you are strong enough to make the thing happen, before that you lack the initiative. And maybe that's why I succumbed on that journey, perhaps that's the place that I found myself in.

For somewhere along that grim roadway my spirits died and, somewhere, I drove into darkness.

I guess the first hint was an abandoned Cortina which had run off the road west of Basildon. They shouldn't have left it there, it should have been cleared away, if they'd done that things might have been different. But it brought back those memories, it hurt, that reminder of it. They really should not have just left it there.

The car seemed undamaged, perhaps it ran out of petrol, perhaps the owner had walked away unscathed. Maybe he intended to return to collect the car, or maybe he'd just grown tired of driving it. Maybe he had stolen it and found himself a new car. Whatever it was, the car was just waiting.

And seeing it like that, at an angle, across a grass verge, it brought back with a jolt how my wife died. It was like a malicious joke, an evil welcome back to my homeland, an indication that only the superficial world changes, while the real world, inside, remains the same. It slapped me clean of whatever mood I'd lapsed into. It sent a dark shiver running through me.

Maybe I was wrong at that point in thinking that I'd cured myself because people often pretend they're much better than they really are, whether their illness is physical or mental. Perhaps I wasn't really as well as I hoped I was, perhaps I had some way to go yet. And also, I'd had a chance to think over many things, driving those hours down the motorway. I'd lost my excitement, I'd had a chance to calm down, my dark seed took its chance to take root again.

Suddenly my homecoming didn't look such a great thing, the plans that I'd made seemed unstable. I'd thought I would go back and explain to the squatters that they really had to give me my house back. I'd go out to dinner parties and maybe phone Franklyn up and ask him if it's okay to take my job back. I'd say that I'd tried a few things and they hadn't worked out for me; I wanted to pick up my old life.

It seems so naïve, really. Nothing's that simple. I should have known that problems of the mind and spirit are not so easily solved.

The trouble was that my family had been part of the old life, but they could not be part of it now because they weren't there. I had been pretending I was someone else, someone fortified by a love of Susan and strong enough to take up that life and rework it, turn a car wreck from scrap metal into a set of navigational instruments that would show me the way through the dark geography of my soul.

However, I now realised that I hadn't got the devices or the skill enough to do that. The mangled Escort was still torn jagged steel and bent axles, and I had neither forge nor tools nor talent to make anything else of it. The wreck still remained a wreck and I could not cope with that, it dominated parts of my mind.

Suddenly, for what seemed to me a perfectly acceptable reason, I knew that I wanted to die. What Susan had given me was not the strength to live, but the strength that I needed to kill myself. At that moment nothing seemed quite so important as putting myself through that last hurdle. And this thought occurred to me as I drove on the same road my own family drove on and died upon.

Half a mile ahead of me the deathstump waited patiently. I'd never done anything to really try to get rid of it, and this was perhaps my undoing. I should have grown angry with it and tried to uproot the thing, but I didn't, I waited until this point. In this circumstance, driving east towards the stump, I was no longer unsure of its position. I would know that dark killer when I saw it.

And I could settle things for good, one way or the other. Me or the stump, either one of us. All that I needed was courage or madness, and it was the madness which finally took hold of me.

The darkness closed around me like something quite tangible. I shook myself as dogs will shake and put some speed inside me. The car started accelerating, growling as I let it loose - it snarled as it leapt through that darkness. Somewhere up ahead of me the tree stump braced against me. It knew I was coming, with its primitive instincts. Out there in the night, it could sense me. It knew my thoughts, as it knew my intention. It knew every fibre inside me. Maybe it was afraid of me, my urge for retribution. It thought it got away with things, went back to senseless sleeping. But now I was coming, with half a ton of metal. The last act in our grim melodrama.

As it came up to top speed the old Sigma was shrieking. And other things also were shrieking. I was screaming. It is possible the tree stump was also adding its own elongated syllables to this cacophony. It came into the headlights and galloped towards me, a vision of weather-washed hatred. It looked hard and defiant, completely unremorseful, as I swung the car hard off the roadway. The car hit the kerb and with a great jump leapt over it and crunched, bounced and skidded on the grass verge. For a moment it slewed as I threatened to lose control of it, but this time, this time I was determined. I could hear nothing but screams of pure fury, saw nothing but oceans of darkness.

I flung my arm across my face as the stump bounded forward to meet me. The tree stump was roaring at me, its face was a torn mask, I saw fingers and talons and sharp teeth. I thought that it must have torn free from the dirt, for it was rushing straight at me on its leg-roots. Then, at the last second, it heard what I screamed at it, and it tried to escape from my fury. It tried to avoid me, to dart through the hedgerow, to dive through my moment of suicide.

'Die you bastard!' I was screaming, and the tree was crying strange things in my direction. Blood spurted out of it - the blood of my family - sprayed over my windscreen like liquid mud. It wanted to blind me, tried hard to enshroud itself, and I could taste its fear, feel its blind terror like a fountain in the night. I almost felt sorry for it as my car leapt upon it, savage and unyielding - ripping and tearing and grinding. Maybe it even begged for my forgiveness, pleaded in that last desperate moment. Maybe it shrieked out in alien accents, 'Oh God, I am *sorry. Please...*' but I had no time for words, of any language, which did not translate into DEATH.

Too late for reason then, my car pounded into it, and in mayhem and blindness I destroyed that rogue stump.

I gave a great scream as the car blew apart on me, and as it ripped from the tree and spun back on the roadway, I encountered a moment of darkness. But that was just a fleeting thing, and the world spun around and the car cried out to me, and the road squealed and I shouted and darkness returned again and through the darkness I saw the lights of cars which were tumbling after me, cars twisting and bouncing my way, all spinning and burning and searing that darkness - and a noise in my ears like a dull thudding, and nothing but crying and broken glass, a wrenching in my chest and the dripping of water, and then - just a terrible silence.

And the silence was broken by voices and motor cars and vision came back to me, swirled away, lost again. Darkness and flashlights and a glow like night bleeding and - 'What in the fuck's going on?' I said.

'Just be quiet. Don't say anything.'

And I didn't want to be quiet because I thought I might be dying and I wanted to make some last fuss before I went, but I couldn't find the strength in me to cry out. And darkness kept coming and plunging me into it, then spitting me out like a grape-pip. It struck me that my last act of taking my own life had failed like I'd failed in so many things. But some failures hurt you and some make you strong again and, this time, I was glad that I'd failed. When it came to the crunch (and it had, in a big way) I was glad I could still draw a breath in me. All this was going through my head in those seconds and I didn't want to die then and I didn't want to hurt any more, and I really just wanted to sleep awhile.

'Am I really going to die?' I asked.

'You won't play the piano for a while.' Which was a joke, but I did not feel too much like laughing about it. Although, on second thoughts, I did start to snigger.

'Why won't I play the piano?' I asked.

He didn't answer because we'd got it the wrong way around. It was me that was supposed to say, 'Will I be able to play the piano?' He must have got it wrong because he was scared - scared that I was dying and he was there to witness this terrifying last act of a living creature.

He said, 'You've smashed both your hands up.'

'But my chest hurts.'

'That's because you keep talking.'

'I'll shut up a while.'

'That's a good idea.'

'Are you a doctor?'

'No, I'm afraid I'm a hairdresser.'

But at least that is something, and if all else should fail me, I could die with a beautiful hairstyle.

But they didn't let me die, people came and looked after me and, strangely, I found myself glad of it. The final battle had been fought and surely, from there on, it was simply a matter of growing stronger and getting myself better. As the body healed, surely the spirit would heal along with it? That's the way I saw it then, as I lay in that bed between crisp white sheets, waited on by the nursing sorority.

DOG PEOPLE: TWENTY ONE

Don't let people talk you into dying, there are too many things to find out still. If you die it's all over, there's no second chance for it, dying's for when there is no hope left. And even then I should think there's some hope left.

I was the one who had talked me into dying, in a quick conversation along the A127, and I was stupid enough just then to believe me. Fortunately, other people saw fit to save me. Fortunately, they're smarter than I am.

What a year, though, I had been through, what a mad time it had been: my family dead, my life invaded, taken over, my home abandoned; Monica lost, my friends, my colleagues, Franklyn, Malcolm all of them gone now, no more invitations to dinner parties. I had lived like a lost hound, performed like a squatter and finally, laughingly, offered to kill myself on the altar of the god I had leaned towards. Nothing but craziness. Utter simplicity. But what a strange year I had lived through.

Plenty of time for these things to be thought about, in a bed, in a ward at the hospital. I sit bolt upright (this is important) to help the crack in my sternum repair itself. And I don't move my hands much because I have little use for them, trapped as they are in thick plaster as far as the elbow. A great deal of plaster for two broken thumb bones; but, fortunately, it's not on much longer. And then I breathe slowly, for my pneumothorax, which in plain terms means half of my lung was deflated (but that gradually gets itself reflated). And apart from a whiplash I've no other injuries, and they tell me I've been very lucky.

I believe them. I never really wanted to die, I just ran out of plans I could live for, and only in a fleeting sense, in another few miles they'd have come back to me. *Don't act too hastily,* that's my new motto. *Don't test your car out on a tree stump.*

I've been here three days now, and all of the nurses know my name, and all of the nurses are kind to me. They don't know that I wanted, in that moment, to kill myself, they think the car crashed when its brakes failed. I don't really mind that for it's not such a big lie, for really it was just that my own brakes failed. I do feel some guilt for occupying this hospital bed, but weighed against that is the fact that I like it here. It's nice to be looked after, it's good to feel safe at last. I just have a problem with urinating.

But at least I feel whole again, back to my old self. I think my last ghost has been busted. Maybe I needed a time like the one I am having, away from the pressures of real life. It's hard to find time sometimes, too many projects, too many vital inconsequences. It could be that everyone should go through a car crash, just to taste death, and recover from it. Death doesn't taste good, and recovery is painful, but you find that you're never alone in it. The Night Sister, Jacqueline, the one we're all in love with, she's a bit smarter than the rest of them. She knows what I did, she knows that I plumped for death, but she also made that choice herself once. She once had a boyfriend and when it was over she took fifty pills in the bathroom. Her father discovered her and, like me, they pulled her back and now, she doesn't even know what he looked like. It just seemed important then, and maybe it was then, just to help get her life into balance.

It seems to me that Jacqueline is aware of a lot of things. That's one thing I've recognised through my travels.

I didn't know anything. I thought when you lose something there's nothing to do but spend the rest of your life brooding over it. I've seen no revelation, I won't dedicate myself to life, but I think there is more to our time here. The spark that was Angela should not fade away for ever, I should take a small part of her onwards. But not in a grim way, and not to be maudlin; no effigies, no gravestones, just living.

All very serious stuff, I consider, and I'll probably forget it all later. I might take up arguing again, shouting at strangers. I'm just going to have myself a good time.

And if I slip back again, well, what does it matter? We weren't meant to have life too easy.

Today, to help me with my recovery, I had my only visitor, a man that I thought I'd forgotten, but he came to me furtive and bashful.

I have had no visitors since I came here (nobody even knows that I am here). I watch other people's and share in their pleasure. And nobody minds that I smile at them.

But today came a dog person, peeping through doorways and frowning and trying to find my bed. He carried a basket filled up with dried flowers which I recognised as stolen from my bathroom. He had one of my coats on, and had probably shaved himself with the spare shaver I keep in my bedroom. He smiled when he finally saw me.

'Hello John,' I said, when he moved to my bedside.

'Hello,' he said shyly. He reached out and touched my shoulder. I remember him doing that. If you're imagining you see people they can't touch you, can they? That's my understanding of the way these things work. You can see and hear them, but not feel them.

'Do you mind if I sit down?'

'No. Pull up that chair, it makes me feel awkward having you tower over me. I feel like a kid in his sick-bed.'

'How are you feeling?'

'Better,' I said. 'Much better. How are things going for you?'

'Not too bad. Better than you I think.'

'Tell me the things you've been up to.'

He shrugged, looking nervous. 'This and that. We've been getting the house ready for you.'

'How did you know I was here?'

'I saw your car. It's still on the roadside, they just moved it out of the way of the traffic.'

'How are the others?'

'We're drifting apart now. After the baby died it wasn't the same. We didn't have anything to keep us there.'

I nodded. 'I wondered. I wondered what went on. I didn't know the relationship between you.'

'A temporary thing. It's all over now.' He put the basket on my bedside cupboard and helped himself to a glass of my water. 'Theresa left, a week or two back now. Then Michael went, and now I'm about ready.'

'Pamela,' I said. 'Her real name is Pamela. I suppose you and Michael have real names too.'

'Yes, I suppose we do,' he conceded.

I was concerned for him.

'Where will you go to?'

He shrugged. 'I don't know. There's always someplace. I might head on down to the south coast.'

'Will you meet up with the others?'

He looked at his massive hands. 'I don't think so. I think that it's over now. It was the baby that bound us, now that that's left us we'll go back to finding our own lives. I'm glad that you helped us - '

'I'm glad that you helped me,' I said.

'There aren't many people who would have done that. Anyway,' he said, 'we've tidied the place up, and we did a few repairs round the property. I think you'll find most things the way that you left them. Although one or two things have been altered. And I'm afraid that we took a few things away with us.'

'That's okay,' I said. 'They're not important.'

'I'm sorry about your accident,' he murmured.

'That's okay, it was only a part of it.'

'And I'm sorry for all of the trouble we caused you.'

'Believe me, it wasn't any trouble.' I put my bandaged hand on his shoulder. 'It was really one of the best things that could have happened.'

'Anyway, we're all of us grateful. It helped us make sense of things.'

'I used to think - ' I hesitated to say it, I didn't know how he'd react to it. 'I used to think it was like having dogs around.'

'I know that.' He smiled at me. 'We are the Dog People. But dogs need to have a pack leader. Once that goes, there's nothing to hold them together. You're the leader, but - you're not a dog, you see.'

'No,' I said. 'I'm only human. I guess that's why you came in the house. Looking for somewhere that she could give birth in. Later, it's no longer necessary.'

There was a moment of silence, and then John said, 'I'd better be getting along now.'

'I know,' I said. 'And - the very best of luck to you.'

And then he just walked away smiling.

After that there was nothing but getting my strength back, and watching my wounds gradually heal themselves. It wasn't too difficult: my lungs filled with air again and the crack in my sternum repaired itself. I watched as my bruises turned purple, then yellow, then faded away to a dull brown. A loose tooth fell out of me and now there's a gap there where my tongue rests when I'm being thoughtful. But I'm not really thoughtful, I'm just waiting through things, I'm waiting to see what will happen.

I might write to Franklyn, see if I can get my old job back; on the other hand, I might try something different. I'm not really a stupid bloke, I should be able to do something. I might get a dog to keep me company.

The only thing bothering me is when I go out of this place, going back to my home on my own. I've had no further visitors and I'm a little embarrassed about explaining to people what I've been through. But, maybe I'll start trying to find some new people, there's a whole world of people out there for me. And if it's a small world, and I end up just living in one tiny backwater that runs through it - it won't really matter, I know from my own pond that all life can fit in one raindrop.

I'm feeling much stronger now, I want to get out of here. I'm eager to face what's in store for me.

DOG PEOPLE: TWENTY TWO

No tomorrow should have to be lonely, and I'm fortunate that I didn't have to face one. For just as I waited for a taxi to collect me, an old friend walked in at the main door.

I was sitting in reception with my things in a brown bag, and I thought I must have looked kind of pitiful: a man with his hands bound and all his belongings, and no one to come to collect him. Everyone had a someone, the kids and the old folk, it was just me who stood around like a stranger.

But Monica was smiling as she reached out her hands to me.

'It's all right, I've come to take you home now.'

'Home,' I said curiously, as I stepped from her Astra.

'You'll be all right now. I'll look after you. You've been through a bad time.'

'Yes,' I said thoughtfully. And so had the others: John, and Michael, and Theresa who had become Pamela. They'd been through a bad time. We'd all had it pretty rough, thinking about it, one way or another.

'Home,' I repeated, and looked at the woodland and suddenly found thoughts returning to me.

Where was the woman who owned those small bones? They were hers. They had been formed inside her. Did I dare take a spade and exhume them? No, I could not do that, I didn't have the courage. And maybe they would not be there now. It would not prove anything. She could have exhumed them before she went off again. They were hers, they were not mine to play with.

Then I thought I heard Monica say, I didn't want to tell you before now, but you may well have a housing problem. The council wants to turn this place into a park. There's a compulsory purchase order on the house and garden. But you can always move in with me, Steven.

The blow was not that I would be homeless.

They'll be digging all of this up then? I murmured.

I suppose so, I heard her voice answer.

I nodded. I would never be able to find the squatters again. I didn't even find out their surnames. It was Pamela's not mine, but I had been left with it. Would they ever believe it was hers?

Monica and I were both silent for a long while, just standing and looking at the wind caught in the trees and trying madly to shake itself free of them. Then I turned to Monica and said, Is that true?

And Monica said, I don't know. It might be.

Printed in Great Britain
by Amazon

26493999R00098